“It’s very late,” [illegible] e window, nothing cou[illegible] 1. Philip could not leave [illegible] el for a man on his own, even one as formidable as [illegible]s. “Will you sleep here tonight?” she asked, sounding breathless.

“Rose.” The use of her name made her all warm inside. When she finally dared to look at him, the warmth became a blazing hot fire. “If I stay here, I am not at all sure I will sleep,” he finished with a growl.

“Nor will I,” she answered in the same tone. No. She would not sleep.

Or at least, not alone.

Rose could have told herself she was grateful for what he had done, that her mind was addled, her judgment altered by today’s unexpected events, but she did not want to lie to herself thus. She was grateful, of course, more than she had ever been in her life, but the truth was that she wanted Philip to make love to her more than anything else in the world. In this moment he wasn’t the man who had given her son back to her, he was the lover who had inflamed her body and who was looking at her with fiery eyes, ready to take her to bed.

She heard herself gasp in anticipation of his touch.

Shadows in the Mist

by

Virginie Marconato

This is a work of fiction. Names, characters, places, and incidents are either the product of the author's imagination or are used fictitiously, and any resemblance to actual persons living or dead, business establishments, events, or locales, is entirely coincidental.

Shadows in the Mist

Contact Information: info@thewildrosepress.com

Cover Art by *The Wild Rose Press, Inc.*

The Wild Rose Press, Inc.
PO Box 708
Adams Basin, NY 14410-0708
Visit us at www.thewildrosepress.com

Publishing History
First Edition, 2023
Trade Paperback ISBN 978-1-5092-4714-1
Digital ISBN 978-1-5092-4715-8

Published in the United States of America

Prologue

England, Summer 1462

Heart beating loudly in her chest, Rose waited.

How long until he came? Not too long, she hoped. Not that she was desperate to be bedded, but as Sir Gilbert had made it clear he was going to come to her tonight, she would rather not spend another moment agonizing over the prospect. The idea of spending the night in his arms was enough to make her blood curdle, but she had no choice.

It had been part of the bargain.

She had promised to allow him her favors, and now she had to honor her word. There would be no wedding otherwise.

Lying on her side with her face averted from the door, she waited. Through the narrow slit window, the sky was black and impenetrable. Not a single ray of light filtered into the room and, as she had been careful to snuff her candle earlier on, Rose could not even see her own hands wringing in anguish.

It was better this way, she told herself. She couldn't have borne to witness Sir Gilbert's triumphant smirk when he positioned himself over her and took possession of her body.

What would Henry say if he could see what she was reduced to doing? How would he handle the knowledge that his actions had unwittingly led her to this pass? Because of his ill-fated decision to support the old king in his battle for the crown, she was now forced to accept another man's attentions to stave off poverty and, more importantly, get their son back. She shook her head to chase the grim thoughts away. Her beloved husband had been dead for nigh on eighteen months now, but the pain of his loss was still searing. Still, she couldn't think about him now, or about Edward. If she did, she would get up and leave before Sir Gilbert came to find her.

The temptation to do so was overwhelming. She could leave. There had to be some other way she had not thought of to get her son back. Anything would be better than allowing a man to take her to bed when her whole body rebelled at the idea. Perhaps something had eluded her, perhaps she could try to…

The door opened with an ominous creak.

Too late. Sir Gilbert would never let her go before he had claimed his prize. She bit her tongue, muffling a cry of despair.

He was not carrying any candles. For a brief moment, the glow of the torch burning in the staircase lit the room, but as soon as the door closed, the darkness was once more complete. Rose heard him getting undressed and gulped. Would he keep his shift on like she had? She dearly hoped so.

The bed sagged when he finally lay next to her. Only when he had to grope around to find her did Rose realize she had moved to the far side of the bed. The message was clear. She didn't want to be here. Screwing her eyes shut, she waited for him to make the first move. She was in the bed. He could not ask for more. She could not have pretended to welcome him, and he probably did not expect her to. As long as she did not fight him off, they could both pretend she was here willingly. This was probably why he was not carrying any light, why he had not addressed her so much as a single question. He did not want to see the anguish on her face, and he did not want to hear the reluctance in her voice.

A hand landed on her shoulder, and a body molded itself against hers. She could not repress a gasp when she realized that her hopes had been vain.

Dear God, he *was* naked.

"You are cold, my sweet," a voice purred at her ear. "Let us see if we can warm you up."

Rose's eyes flew open.

The seductive tone of voice had taken her by surprise. Sir Gilbert was not a man she would have cited for his gentleness. Then again, their acquaintance was short, and she had never heard him whisper before, much less while he was lying in bed next to her, trying to entice her into lovemaking. He took her in his arms and nuzzled at the crook of her neck, rubbing his cheek against her invitingly. Then the hand at her shoulder stole to her front and came to cup her breast. Two fingers started to play with her nipple, which became rock hard under the unexpected caress.

"Mmm, still cold I see, lady. Or is it something else?"

He gave a soft laugh Rose was shocked to find arousing. The hand at her breast became even more persuasive, stroking, squeezing gently, handling her with a delicacy of touch she had always assumed men only used with the women they loved. Evidently she had been wrong, for she knew full well it was not love Sir Gilbert felt for her.

The hand slid downward and stayed on her stomach a while, warm and comforting. With his fingers splayed on her belly, he drew her closer to him, and she felt against the small of her back the hard proof of his desire for her. Her cheeks burst into flames, and she gave a strangled cry.

At the sound, he gave another laugh.

"Come, I daresay you are just as hot for me," he breathed, and to her utmost confusion, he slid his hand between her thighs to cup her intimately. His fingers danced on her soft flesh, and Rose could not prevent a sound of longing from escaping her lips. It had been so long since a man had stroked her in that way that she could not help the treacherous response of her body. It ignited in longing, urging her to relent.

"Yes, just as I thought. You cannot lie to me, my sweet." The voice became even huskier. Rose closed her eyes again and understood that she would not stop him now.

The fingers carried on with their caress, and soon she found herself panting in pleasure. The man was skilled, unexpectedly so, and suddenly she could not remember why she should be resisting his caresses. It felt so good to be touched by a man in this way.

The hem of her shift was lifted to her waist to give him better access to her most intimate parts. Rose let out a series of shaky breaths. By now she was all but writhing against him, all shame forgotten. Her body was on fire, demanding the release it had been denied for so long.

As if he had guessed her need, he entered her, almost without moving. His fingers had not stopped their relentless exploration for a moment. Once he had filled her, he stayed still and groaned his satisfaction. Rose whimpered. It felt so right… She had never imagined she would actually want him to move inside her, but oh, she did—she was desperate for it.

So desperate she arched her back to force him deeper inside.

"Oh, I see!" He laughed. "You want more." He eased himself out of her, excruciatingly slowly, stilling his hand as well, denying her the stimulation she craved. Frustration welled within her. Surely he was not going to stop now? "Tell me you want me," he purred.

"I…"

She could not say it; it would have been a lie. She did not want *him*. She wanted *this*, which was not the same thing at all. Her body was playing tricks on her, relishing a man's caresses after going so long without. Her deprived senses had been won over by his assured touch, and between them they had silenced the protests in her mind. Rose had never imagined Sir Gilbert would be a skillful lover, but she could not fool herself any longer. He'd had her panting in pleasure in no time, and she was now grinding her hips against him shamelessly, asking for more.

The thought turned her cheeks red with mortification, but she was unable to control herself. He was poised behind her, hard, ready to slide back inside her, and in that moment she would have done anything for him to resume his caresses.

"Please," was all she said, the word barely more than a whisper.

He grunted as if this was the response he had been waiting for. Without asking for more, he filled her again with one long, easy stroke. His fingers resumed his teasing, and soon Rose felt a wave of unstoppable pleasure wash over her. For a delicious moment she remained on the edge of ecstasy, and then one nip at her neck pushed her over into the abyss. She cried out loud in a voice she had never heard before. Henry had never coaxed such a shocking response from her. Bewildered, she realized that what she had experienced at the hands of this man she despised had surpassed all the delights she had enjoyed in the arms of her beloved husband.

She would have recoiled in shame and self-loathing, but she was unable to move, her body had gone liquid with satisfaction. Behind her, she was dimly aware of Sir Gilbert moving, changing positions.

"Well, my sweet, let us see if we can make you give that delicious cry again."

Rose did not have time to answer. In the blink of an eye she found herself under a taut body and a soft mouth that made her forget everything.

Chapter 1

"For shame, you are nothing but the worst kind of slut!"

Rose's eyes flickered open at the venom in Sir Gilbert's voice. Had he really just called her a slut? It certainly seemed so, but she had difficulty focusing. Finally she opened her eyes. Standing by the bed, staring at her with a look of affronted pride on his face, was Sir Gilbert. It took her a moment to understand why the fact surprised her so. Her mind was hazy, her limbs strangely limp. Then she saw he was fully dressed, with a candle in his hand, when the last thing he'd done before falling asleep was roll off from her pulsing body, weakened by the intensity of his release.

Something wasn't right.

"How did you…?" she mumbled, turning to her side where he should be. The rest of the question was lost in a horrified gasp.

A man was indeed on the bed next to her. A hand proprietorially closed over her breast, he was sleeping soundly, sprawled on his stomach, naked. It did not take Rose long to understand that *he* had been the one making love to her only a few moments ago.

Sir Gilbert had evidently reached the same inescapable conclusion.

"You had the gall to bring your lover here when you knew I would be coming to you?" He let out a snarl that would never pass for the laugh it was supposed to be. “By God, I don’t know if I should admire your boldness or be scandalized by your duplicity and wantonness.”

Rose hastily gathered the sheet to cover herself. She was still naked, exposed to his gaze. Fortunately he seemed too irate to make the most of this opportunity to ogle her. “It’s not what…”

He raised a hand, cutting her protests short. “If you are about to say that this is not what it looks like, then you can save your breath. This is exactly what it looks like.”

Privately Rose had to admit he had a point. The man in the bed with her was holding her in an intimate embrace, he was sleeping like someone half dead from exhaustion, and his hair was still damp with sweat. They were both naked, and the sheets around them were crumpled from their energetic lovemaking.

Indeed, there was no room for misinterpretation.

She must have been asleep only for a moment, for her body was still throbbing from the mind-blowing pleasure the man had given her. With her lips swollen from their kissing and her breast in his hand, she would present a picture of such lasciviousness that there was no hope of ever convincing Sir Gilbert she was innocent of any wrongdoing.

She would never be able to talk her way out of this.

“I will see you tomorrow at dawn,” Sir Gilbert said coldly. “When you are in a more seemly state. But I think we can both agree that our arrangement is off.”

He strode away before Rose could reply, leaving her numb with confusion and shame.

****

Philip Whitlock, newly made Lord Chrystenden,

was wakened by a resounding slap. He swore and sat up in the bed, ready to face his opponent—only to find no one in front of him.

"Who are you?" a woman asked from the other side of the bed, anger audible in her rasping voice. He turned to face her.

"Did you just slap me?" he asked in incredulity, rubbing at his jaw.

The question was unnecessary. There was no one else in the room, and her face was dark with fury. It had to have been her. But why? What had he done to provoke her ire?

She was a young woman and, incongruously, she was wearing a dark blue mantle, the sort you would only wear to go outside, not in a room in the middle of the night. What's more, he could tell from the glimpse of skin at her throat that she was naked underneath. A guest at the castle, she must have entered his room by mistake and found him in bed. Her unusual state of undress made it clear she had been wandering around in search of her lover—and found him instead. That still didn't explain why she would have slapped him for doing nothing more damning than sleep in his own bed.

He surveyed her quickly.

Whoever she had gone to find, he was a lucky man. With a tangle of curls cascading down her shoulders and her full, red mouth, she was quite something to look at. Her huge, innocent eyes were of a shape he had only ever seen in does before, but instead of being brown, hers were deep blue, the color offering a pleasing contrast to the pink cheeks that made her appear younger than she probably was.

To complete this picture of loveliness, a dusting of

freckles graced her small, upturned nose. The heavy garment she was wearing only made him desperate to see what was concealed underneath. Curves to die for, probably, and skin as smooth as cream.

Incredibly, Philip felt his manhood stir. You would have thought it had had enough for one night, but looking at the woman's angelic face—and imagining the voluptuous body hidden under the mantle—made it come alive. He gave an amused snort. Really, he was incorrigible! Only a moment ago he had exhausted himself by taking Lady Hershey twice, and here he was, lusting after the mysterious guest.

He frowned. Something was bothering him, but he could not put his finger on it, and the woman was too distracting to allow him to think straight.

Whatever it was, it would have to wait. First he had to deal with his unexpected visitor. She had just slapped him, and he still had no idea why. Philip did not like to be left in the dark about anything.

"I usually try to get to know women better before I let them abuse me, and even then they have to ask *very* nicely beforehand," he drawled, unable to resist the temptation to tease her. She had been looking for a man and she had just found one. Could he not persuade her to stay a bit longer? His manhood gave a twitch, as if to nod its agreement. "But I could make an exception for you."

He had hoped she would respond in a similar style, but he quickly saw from the thunderous expression on her face that seduction was the last thing on her mind. In fact, she looked ready to lash out at him.

The comment was so outrageous Rose barely resisted the urge to slap the man again. Was he really suggesting that they fall into bed yet again? She was beside herself with fury, and the shocking offer did nothing to appease her anger. All her efforts had been ruined by that man, and instead of repenting he had the gall to tease her and look at her as if he was about to ravish her.

For the third time.

Well, it would not happen! After Sir Gilbert left the room, her first instinct had been to rouse the man and shake him until he gave her an explanation for his presence in her bed, but she had taken the time to light a candle first and, even more importantly, put some clothes on. Not for the world did she want to confront him naked.

Just as she was placing the candle holder onto the chest, he had rolled over onto his back. Her mantle had been the first thing she'd found to cover her nudity. She'd hastily thrown it onto her shoulders and then…

Then she had been unable to move.

Whoever he was, the man lying on his back in such an abandoned pose was…spectacular. His long limbs were sculpted to perfection, his hands supremely elegant, his muscles firm under a skin the color of honey. The sight had taken her breath away. Every part of him was flawless, and she could not detach her gaze from the sight in front of her.

Still, magnificent as he was, he had just destroyed all her hopes of being reunited with her son.

Before she had time to think the better of such an action, Rose had slapped him as hard as she could, fury and powerlessness overwhelming her. This man had just ruined her life, and had she had access to a sword in that moment, she might well have slashed at him with it.

"Who are you?" she repeated, feeling on the verge of hysterics. "What are you doing here?"

Everything slammed back into place in Philip's mind. Now that he was properly awake, he realized what had been bothering him all this time. He was alone in the bed.

He should most definitely not be alone, not considering what had happened only moments before.

"Who are *you*?" he asked instead of answering. "And what are you doing in my room? Where is Lady Hershey?"

"Who on earth is Lady Hershey?"

Rose was now the one on the back foot. She had not expected the man to be surprised at finding someone he didn't know in the room. By now she had half convinced herself he had been sent to her by Sir Gilbert so he could have an excuse to go back on his word, or even just in a perverted sexual game. Evidently she had been wrong. The man's surprise was not feigned. He truly seemed to have no idea who she was and what she was doing here.

Though it was the last thing Rose should be worrying about, when he frowned she found herself wondering if his eyes were black or just a very dark shade of brown.

"Lady Hershey is the woman who was in my bed a moment ago," he said patiently, looking at her as if she was a simpleton.

A horrible suspicion invaded Rose. He had just said that this was his room. Could he really be saying what she thought he was saying?

"The woman you made love to?" she asked in a deathly whisper. "Twice?"

His eyes narrowed further. They were not quite black she decided, more a liquid, velvety brown. Fascinating.

"How could you possibly know this?" he asked slowly.

"Because that woman was me, not Lady Hershey."

Philip rubbed the bridge of his nose and closed his eyes. Had he been hit harder than he'd thought? Nothing he was being told made any sense. "You? I made love to *you*?"

"Yes. There has been a misunderstanding," the woman said hurriedly. "I was in the bed when you arrived. You must have thought I was the lady you were expecting."

He almost laughed out loud at this explanation. Did she really expect him to believe such a ludicrous thing? The mysterious beauty had a wicked sense of humor! Then he saw her wring her hands in despair, and the laughter died in his throat. She wasn't teasing him; she was mortified and furious all at once. He blinked. There was only one reason for her to feel that way.

Because she was telling the truth.

"Yes. I admit that I did take you for Lady Hershey," he said, titling his head, not quite sure if he should be aghast at this development or amused. "Why didn't you correct my mistake and throw me out of the bed?"

Rose hesitated. Loath as she was to tell him what had happened, she had to justify herself, otherwise he would question her morals—if not her sanity. She was effectively saying that she had not thought anything of a man she didn't know coming to her bed naked and making love to her. What sort of a woman would behave in such a way?

A woman she did not wish to be mistaken for, that was who.

"I… I was waiting for someone. It was dark, and I

thought you were him."

For a long moment Philip stayed silent. Then the laughter he had tried so hard to contain escaped his throat.

"Yes, well, it makes perfect sense now. If you were waiting for a man to come join you in bed, then of course you didn't jump out of your skin when one did just that!" He crossed his arms on his chest, highly entertained. "But I was not your lover, and you were not Lady Hershey. Come to think of it, I did think you were oddly restrained for a woman who had all but assaulted me the day before. At least *at first* I did," he amended, throwing her a piercing stare. "I quickly stopped wondering."

Indeed it had not taken her long to surrender to his caresses and come undone. His body jerked in remembrance, and he smiled at her.

Rose felt her cheeks grow hot. The man laughed again, the soft laugh she remembered from earlier. It was a sound that could both arouse and soothe. Then she remembered the scathing way Sir Gilbert had talked to her, accusing her of being the worst kind of slut and calling off their wedding.

It had been the most humiliating moment of her existence, even if she had endured more painful ones.

"How can you laugh?" she cried out. "It was awful!"

"Thank you," Philip said dryly. "I do not remember hearing any complaints earlier. Neither the first nor the second time."

She shot him what she probably meant to be a withering look, but she succeeded only in making his lips quiver. The woman was…adorable. The incongruous thought made his smile broaden. Since when did he think of women as adorable?

“How did you not realize I was not the woman you meant to bed?” she demanded crossly, unaware she was endearing herself to him more with every passing moment.

“My acquaintance with Lady Hershey is very short. We only met yesterday at my friend the Comte de Maudile’s castle when, as I just told you, she shamelessly begged me to make love to her,” he explained. “She lured me to the stables. I asked her to come to my bed if only she could wait another day, having absolutely no intention of taking her over offensive-smelling, dirty straw. You can see now why I was not surprised to find a willing woman in my bed, for I had arranged it to be so. More to the point, how did you not recognize your lover?”

“He’s not my lover!” Rose immediately rebelled at the notion. “We have never…lain together before.”

“You still haven’t,” the man pointed out with infuriating logic. An amused light was dancing in his eyes. In fact, since he had found out she was not this Lady Hershey, he had not stopped smiling, as if this was the most entertaining adventure that could have happened to two people. But Rose was not amused in the least. If he had no idea of the cataclysmic repercussions the night’s events would have, she certainly did.

He had destroyed the first ray of hope she’d had in months, and she was not inclined to be generous.

“I don’t see how you can laugh,” she all but screamed. “And would it be too much to ask you to cover yourself up while we are talking?” She gestured at the naked torso on display in front of her. Mercifully he had covered his lap, but the sheet still allowed her to see the trail of dark hair on his taut stomach and even that was too intimate for comfort. The only other naked stomach she had ever seen was Henry's.

He glanced at his lap, and Rose could not help but blush.

She hadn't seen the man when he had made love to her, but she had felt him, and now that she thought about it rationally, she realized she should have known something was amiss. This was the body of a warrior in his prime. Sir Gilbert, who was renowned for his idleness, could never have felt so hard and muscular. Even in his clothes you could detect the beginnings of a paunch, and his shoulders were nowhere near as broad or strong. This man was to Sir Gilbert what a mighty fortress was to a crumbling peasant's cottage.

His undeniable appeal, however, did not change the fact that he had just ruined her life.

She bunched her fists to stop herself from crying. Once she was alone, she would collapse, but not yet, not in front of him.

"I want you gone," she told him as peremptorily as she dared. He still had made no effort to cover himself, as if he had no idea how tempting his naked body was—or did not care about the embarrassment he was causing her.

"You are forgetting you are in my room," he said with a tilt of the head. "If anyone should leave, it is you."

There was nothing she could answer to that. He was right. If this was truly his room, she should be the one to leave. But where would she go? She did not know the castle well enough to be able to find an alternative sleeping place, and the idea of wandering around in the cold, dressed only in her mantle, was enough to make her howl in despair. She would be seen, and then what?

Rose looked around her helplessly. Her gown was on the chest where she had left it, but her shift was nowhere to be found. It probably lay in a dark corner of the room, where it had landed after being flung there in haste. The man had taken it off her before making love to her a second time, whispering that he was dying to kiss her breasts. His touch had inflamed her so much it had been impossible to say no.

She let out a whimper at the memory of his lips on her heated skin, exploring every inch of her aching breasts, suckling her nipples into tight little buds and making her pant with need.

Dear Lord, what had she done? She should have gotten up and left the room there and then. By then Sir Gilbert had had what he wanted, or so she'd thought, so she had held her side of the bargain. She should never have agreed to the man's request, for inevitably it had led to more. Once he had kissed her breasts, neither he nor she had been in a mood to leave it there. He had positioned himself between her thighs as naturally as if they had made love a thousand times, and taken her again.

She had been far too aroused to protest, and now she would spend the rest of her life paying for this moment of folly.

"I don't know what to do or where to go," she said in a small voice, utterly defeated now that all her hopes of being reunited with Edward had gone.

She could not go to Sir Gilbert. Even supposing she wanted to, after what had transpired between her and the man, he would hardly welcome her, presuming her a slut. And she could not go to sleep in the great hall half naked for everyone to gawp at!

With a sigh, the man ran a hand through his hair, ruffling it even further. Oddly, it did not take away from his beauty. Anyone else would have looked slovenly in such a state, but he only contrived to look more appealing, as if this hint of wildness matched his true nature.

Would she have felt even worse if the man who'd bedded her by mistake had not been such a model of masculine beauty, Rose wondered? Given the nature of the misunderstanding, it could very well have happened. She had not accepted him in her bed because of the appeal he exerted over her but because she thought she had no choice. He could have been anyone, and frighteningly ugly.

But there was nothing frightening or ugly about the man in front of her. Quite the opposite. Had she met him in any other circumstances, she would not have hesitated in calling him the most alluring man she had ever met. Handsome as he had been, Henry had not possessed any of this raw power. The shocking, disloyal thought only made her more furious.

How could she even compare the two men! She had loved her husband, and he had loved her!

"Can't you see? I cannot go anywhere!" she cried out. "I am wearing my mantle, but I'm…"

She was naked underneath.

Suddenly she feared she would not be able to contain her tears any longer.

Philip heard the hint of panic in the woman's voice. She was angry, but there was genuine anguish in her blue eyes, and he could tell she was on the verge of tears. The whole event had shaken her badly.

Remorse, not a sentiment he was prone to feel, filled

him.

"Listen," he said more gently. "You stay here for the night. I shouldn't have been at the castle tonight, and after all, you were here before me. I will find another room."

He got out of bed before she could avert her eyes. Unable to resist the temptation of seeing the expression on her face when she saw him naked, he had not warned her he was about to stand up. Her reaction didn't disappoint. With her innocent blue eyes and flushed cheeks, she looked like an angel, but one about to commit a carnal sin—and she did not look away…

For good measure, he stretched, feeling more alive than he had in a long time.

Rose's jaw dropped open at the sight of the man's body displayed so impudently in front of her. At least she hoped it was shock, and not…

Longing.

The notion tore through her mind. She desired this man! Say what she might, she desired him. Moments ago, he had been making love to her, making her cry out in pleasure. Now he was exposing every inch of his glorious body, and all she could think about was how she wanted him to take her into his arms again.

She turned hastily away, and thought she heard him laugh. It infuriated her further. Just because he had made love to her, it did not mean she was ready to see him naked!

"How long does it take to get dressed?" she could not help but snap. The sooner he covered himself up the better.

"I am finished. You can turn around safely now. You won't burst into flames," he replied, his tone mocking. "I will leave you in peace, so you can get some sleep."

"*Sleep*?" Rose scoffed in incredulity. "You really think I am in the mood for sleeping right now?"

"Are you not?" A slow smile stretched his lips. "I can't say I am either. What say you we…"

"Don't you dare say anything!" she cut in fiercely. "Don't you even dare think it!"

A throaty laugh answered her. "Very well, lady, I won't say a word. But I will think whatever the hell I want. And you cannot stop me."

Philip allowed his eyes to wander over her. She truly was exquisite, far more beautiful than Lady Hershey. Pity he had not known who she was when he had made love to her, for it would have made the moment even more special. Not that he could have had much more pleasure. His release had been explosive, more intense than usual, and he could not account for it.

Seeing the way he devoured her with his eyes, Rose gathered the folds of her mantle, wondering if it had not come gaping during their argument and revealed a glimpse of her naked body. She cursed herself for having been in such a hurry to confront him that she had eschewed the retrieval of her shift. In her defense, she had never imagined the man would turn out to be a predatory rogue who would tell her to her face he was imagining what he would do to her!

"Get out!" she hissed, feeling murderous. "Get out before I…"

"Slap me?" he suggested with an arched brow. "You have already done so. And believe me, you won't get away with it a second time."

Rose's eyes narrowed. "I will do far worse than slap

you if I get my hands on you!"

"I am not unduly worried. You getting your hands on me doesn't sound half as unpleasant as you seem to think it will be. But I told you. You will have to ask *very* nicely to be allowed to abuse me."

"You are so…" She was so furious she could not think of a word to do justice to her anger.

"Do not get yourself in such a state. I said I would go, and I will." He dropped her an insultingly low bow. "I bid you good night, my lady."

Rose watched the man walk out of the room and did something she had never thought herself capable of. In a gesture of helpless fury she sent a ewer full of water crashing to the floor.

So all her scheming had come to nothing! Sir Gilbert would never marry her now, and who else would? A woman of four-and-twenty, the widow of a traitor with no connection or money and with a child from her previous marriage, she was not an attractive prospect for anyone in search of a bride.

It was all the man's fault.

His mistake would cost her dearly, whereas he would simply resume his life as if nothing had happened. Before the week was over, he would have bedded scores of other women and thoroughly forgotten her.

She still had no idea who he was. She had been too incensed—and once he had stood in front of her naked, too confused—to ask him anything about his identity. Though they did not look similar in the least, he had to be a member of Sir Gilbert's family. He'd said that this was his room, and he knew the castle well enough to find his way around it without a light. If only he had carried a candle last night and seen who was lying in the bed before he had taken her into his arms! If only she hadn't been so foolish as to wait for Sir Gilbert in the dark! If only…

She gritted her teeth. There was no use crying now. What was done was done. In the morning she would be sent away from Harleith Castle in disgrace. She could not see a way to prevent it.

Unless… Should she go to Sir Gilbert and beg him to listen to her story? It had been a mistake, after all, and she was not the wanton he had accused her of being. Perhaps she could even convince her mysterious lover to confirm her version of events? She had the feeling, however, that it would only make matters worse. Even if Sir Gilbert believed her outrageous story—which, given the improbable nature of it, was far from certain—the fact remained that she had slept with another, fitter, infinitely more handsome man. He would no doubt take exception to that humiliation.

To convince him that she had not realized her mistake, she would have to admit she had waited for him in the dark, had not asked any questions, and had not said a word because she wanted the ordeal to be over as soon as possible.

At first, at least.

Quickly, too quickly, she had lost herself in the pleasure of the man's embrace. It seemed ludicrous now to have imagined this skillful lover to be Sir Gilbert. Not only had his body been that of a warrior in his prime, but his behavior had been nothing like what she had dreaded. He had been gentle without lacking in virility, full of fiery passion without ever making her feel threatened.

Her body gave a quiver at the memory. No. Definitely not threatened, more desired, almost…cherished.

Without having ever lain in Sir Gilbert's arms, she knew instinctively he would never have awakened her senses thus. He would not caress and pleasure his lover; he would take possession of her body as a conqueror took possession of a land he laid claim to. He would not make her moan; he would make her grit her teeth and wait for it to be over with. Rose's gaze landed on the entangled sheets, and she blushed furiously when she remembered how she had behaved. Whoever the man was, he would think her the most shameful wanton. In fact, he had already told her as much.

I thought you were oddly restrained. At least at first *I did. I quickly stopped wondering.*

Silky voice notwithstanding, it was the most insulting comment she had ever heard.

Would he boast about the adventure to his friends? Her reputation would be utterly ruined if he did. Then she realized he did not know her identity, any more than she knew who he was. The relief was short lived, however. If, as she supposed, he was close to Sir Gilbert, it would not be long before he got to hear about the shocking episode and understand that the villain of the piece was none other than himself. Would he take her defense, explaining that it had all been an honest mistake?

Of course he would not.

More than likely he would keep silent rather than risk the wrath of a humiliated Sir Gilbert, but once he was out of here there would be no stopping him from telling everyone of his adventure. He would come out as a hero, possessing an unsuspecting woman twice, and making her cry out in an excess of pleasure despite her initial reluctance.

No one would approach her after this.

Now she would never get the second husband she desperately needed. Not only had he ruined her chances of marrying Sir Gilbert, but he had the power to destroy her good name and make it impossible for any man within a hundred miles to want her. No one wanted a fallen woman for a wife. A new surge of hate swelled inside of her. Had she known where he had disappeared to, she would have gone to find the man and demand his silence about tonight's events. Surely he would not be so heartless as to refuse a lady this favor. His touch had betrayed a thoughtful, generous man, far from the arrogant rogue who had told her to her face that he would imagine her naked if it pleased him, and he might allow her to abuse him if she begged for it first.

One thing was for sure—she would not get any more sleep tonight.

Rose fell onto the bed, utterly defeated. Instead of the tears she was expecting, she felt her heart breaking even more.

This time it was over.

She would never get Edward back.

Chapter 2

"Wait!"

Philip hurried toward the lady, stopping her in the act of placing her foot on the stirrup of a tired-looking horse. It was her, he was sure of it, even though the cascade of blonde hair he had admired the night before was now hidden under a very conservative hairpiece. The mantle… The blue mantle was the same. He felt his body stir at the mere sight of it, even if he guessed that this time she would not be naked underneath the woolen folds.

"Wait, don't go." The way she tensed told him she had recognized his voice. Yes. It was her. He drew up to her side. "We need to talk."

"I don't think so." She tried to hoist herself onto the saddle once more, but he stopped her, taking her waist in his hands. He felt her inhale sharply when he touched her. "Let me go!" she cried. "How dare you put your hands on me!"

"After what we did last night, I didn't think you would object to me holding your waist," he whispered in her ear. He had the satisfaction of feeling her body slump against his. "I see you dressed today… Pity, I would have liked to see what you hide under your mantle."

Rose let out a whimper. Just by putting his hands on her, the wretched man had put paid to her determination. And then, as if that was not enough, his words had reduced her to a liquid mess. How could that be?

"Please, I need to go," she said in a croak. "Sir Gilbert doesn't desire my presence here any longer."

Philip instantly recoiled. A mace blow to the head would not have stunned him more.

"You are here at *Gilbert*'s invitation?" he snapped, turning her to face him. In view of this new information, the desire to tease her had well and truly vanished.

Rose found herself staring deep into the man's eyes, the dark eyes which had bewitched her the previous night. But today they were not melting in desire or even alight with mockery. They were flashing in fury. The hands at her waist tightened; she could feel the fingers digging into her flesh. He was no longer holding her in a sensual caress.

It was as if he was about to lose control and break her in his anger.

"Let me go," she whispered. Suddenly, he scared her. Naked or not, had he looked half as fierce last night, she would have fled the room in fright.

"Answer me," he growled. "Did you come here to see Gilbert?"

White-hot fury blazed through Philip at the thought. Last night she had admitted to having waited for a man. And now she was telling him that she was here as one of Gilbert's guests…

He took her arm and dragged her away from prying ears despite her protests, only stopping once they had reached a secluded spot in the lists.

"Tell me the man you mistook me for yesterday was not Gilbert!" he demanded through gritted teeth, barely managing to formulate the words for sheer anger. She did not answer, but the way she flushed told him it was.

Philip let out a series of loud curses. This woman was Gilbert's lover! Or at least wanted to be. No. It could not be! He shook his head as if that would be enough to make it untrue. The notion was too ludicrous, too painful to be true.

"I did think you were Sir Gilbert," she said in a deathly voice, her eyes huge with anguish. He could tell he was frightening her, and he forced himself to curb his fury.

"Are you his lover?" he asked once he had regained some control.

"No!" she protested, just as she had last night. "I told you, we have never lain together."

"You were waiting for him in bed, you let me take you because you thought I was him," he said, speaking each word with icy deliberation. "I am not the fool you evidently take me for. How do you expect me to believe that you…"

"It's not what you think," Rose interrupted quickly. She realized that she had told Sir Gilbert exactly the same thing the evening before—and that he had not believed her any more than this man did.

"It's not what I think… I would be curious to know what it is, then. What reason could you possibly have to welcome a naked man to your bed if it is not to become his lover?"

"He… We were supposed to be married," she explained in a breath. There was no choice but to tell him the truth now. She could not let him think her the worst kind of wanton, the kind who bedded men indiscriminately.

Married?

Philip had never been the kind of man to be lost for

words, but the announcement left him speechless. Gilbert, who had always made a point of saying only a foolish man would shackle himself to a wife when it would make it more difficult for him to attend to his many conquests, *that* Gilbert was about to be married? The man who wanted nothing more than to sow his wild oats in peace and marry only when he thought it was time to have an heir had changed his mind and was now betrothed to *this* woman, a woman who would be wasted on him?

It was unbelievable.

"I have never heard of you," he said eventually, getting over the shock.

"I am Lady Rose Maltravers. Our union was a rather sudden decision. That's why you wouldn't have heard of it. Only the close family has been told, I think."

The man made a face Rose hesitated in identifying. He seemed torn between devastating fury and… Was it mirth? Whatever it was, it made his eyes gleam dangerously.

"*I* wasn't told about it," he said with a tilt of the head.

"Well, as I said…"

"I know what you said. Still, I haven't heard about this marriage, and I think I would qualify as close family. I am Lord Chrystenden." She blinked, indicating that the name was unfamiliar to her. "The title is new. I earned it on the battlefield last year. You might simply know me as Philip. Gilbert may have mentioned me?"

He bowed and smiled like a man proud of the jest he had just made. But Rose could only stare back in horror, for Sir Gilbert had indeed mentioned a Philip many times. She leaned against the wall for support.

This could not be happening. Soon she would wake up from the whole nightmare.

"Philip. Oh, dear God. You are his brother."

"*Step*brother," the man specified immediately, as if it made all the difference.

"But we…you…"

Her voice died out, but he finished for her. "I made love to you, his intended bride. Yes. I can see why you would be distraught at the idea. That is rather…" His eyes glittered, and this time she had no difficulty identifying the glint as mirth. "Inconvenient."

"*Inconvenient*?" Rose cried out. How could he be so relaxed about it? "It's not inconvenient! It's indecent and shocking! It's a catastrophe. Sir Gilbert came into the room last night after we'd…" She was stammering, such was her anger. "He screamed at me, and said that the wedding was cancelled, that I was a…a slut. You were there, naked, with your hands all over me, and he… Oh, it was awful."

Philip could scarcely believe what Rose was saying. Gilbert had found him in bed with his intended bride? Well, that would have been a blow, probably the worst humiliation he had endured yet. He could not help but smirk at the thought.

"I'm surprised Gilbert did not confront me there and then," he mused out loud. The man would have been beside himself with fury, and rightly so.

"That's because he did not recognize you. You were fast asleep, lying on your stomach with your face hidden. You did not budge an inch all the time he was in the room!" Rose exclaimed, as the shame of the moment washed over her.

"Well, I was rather spent. I think you know why."

The man she now knew as Sir Gilbert's brother flashed her a wicked grin. Evidently he did not comprehend the seriousness of the situation. "Why didn't you wake me? I could have defended you," he said more seriously before she could lash out at him.

"I had no idea who you were, at the time," she argued. Would it even have helped? Would Sir Gilbert have preferred being told his own brother had taken his place in her bed? Somehow she didn't think so. "And he did not give me much time to justify myself. He told me the wedding was off and stormed out of the room."

Philip tried to imagine Rose's reaction at being wakened by her furious groom-to-be only to realize that she was naked next to a complete stranger who had just made love to her. It must have been quite a shock. No wonder she had slapped him. Another pang of remorse seized him. He should have been the one facing Gilbert, not her.

"Even if you didn't know who I was, you should have wakened me. I could have explained the misunderstanding."

She shook her head. "I was too surprised, too distraught. I did not think…"

Philip rubbed the back of his neck. What a muddle! But perhaps it was not all bad news. "Did you say the wedding was cancelled?" he asked, focusing on the positive.

"Yes. When Sir Gilbert saw that I had…" She blushed furiously, as if she could not bring herself to describe what they had done. "Yes. It is cancelled," she finished succinctly.

Good, that was the important thing. Only one last thing was left to establish.

"Do you love him?"

"*Love* him?" The scathing tone was enough to answer his question. She did not. Philip let out a long breath. He could not have borne the idea of this woman being in love with his despicable stepbrother. "No. I do not love him."

"Then why did you…?" The question died on his lips. How could he word it without offending her? Unexpectedly, she came to his rescue.

"Why did I welcome him in bed without a word of protest, you mean?"

He gave a snort. "You have to admit it is hard to believe that any lady would behave in such a way unless she loved the man."

The criticism hit Rose hard, even though she understood what he was saying. Indeed, no lady worthy of the name would ever behave in such a manner.

"Yes, it is hard to believe," she conceded through gritted teeth. "Almost as hard as to believe that you bedded me by mistake. Yet you claim that this is what happened."

Philip's eyes narrowed. "What the devil is that supposed to mean?"

She did not let herself be impressed by the temper threatening to burst through. "As you said, it all seems too extraordinary to be believed. I am now wondering if you did not arrange it all with your brother, just to…"

"I told you, he's not my real brother!" he cut in, taking her by the arm. "And we decidedly do *not* arrange it between ourselves to bed and humiliate women! You would do well to remember that. I did come to you as a mistake, unbelievable as it sounds. As I said, you were in my room, my bed, and I thought you were Lady

Hershey."

"And where is this mysterious lady now? Why did she not come to you as arranged?" Rose was still suspicious. It all seemed so convenient that no one had entered the room last night, looking for the handsome Lord Chrystenden.

"I found out this morning that she was stopped at the entrance of the castle. Apparently the steward mistook her for a woman of little virtue and would not let her in." Philip let out a small laugh. The man didn't know the half of it! "But why were you in my room?" he asked more seriously.

"I had no idea it was yours! I was told to go to the room at the top of the round tower. How was I to know it belonged to someone else?" she defended.

Philip nodded. Indeed, as a guest she would have gone where she was told to go. Trust Gilbert to use the room for his own purpose, however lewd that purpose may be. He would not be surprised if the notion of taking a woman in his despised stepbrother's room had stirred his blood. He would have had the impression of getting one over on him, and as Philip had not announced his arrival, Gilbert would have had no reason to suspect the room would not be available for his bedding of Lady Rose.

He shook his head. The sequence of events of the previous night, however unlikely, had led to him bedding his stepbrother's betrothed and destroying their plans of marriage. That was bad enough, but what if he had also ruined her in the process?

He looked at her in dismay. The idea of having angered Gilbert left him utterly cold, but he could not bear the idea of having done anything to hurt Rose or her reputation. The evening before, when she had wakened him with a resounding slap, he had been mocking, but now he understood the extent of the disaster she was facing.

He had made love to her without knowing who she was or why she was there. It hadn't been his intention, but in doing so he might well have ruined her life.

"Please tell me you were not a virgin before I came to you?" he asked as the idea suddenly crossed his mind. He wouldn't put it past Gilbert to ruin an innocent maiden, especially if he had been intent on marrying her afterward. If he wanted her, he would not have let the question of her maidenhead stop him.

She blushed at the very personal question, as any lady would, but he had to know. He did not think this would be the case, but as he had taken her on the assumption that she was Lady Hershey and not new to the art of lovemaking, he had not tried to be particularly gentle—and he had given her little respite.

"No. I was not a maid. I have been married before," she murmured, easing his conscience. Indeed she had not felt or behaved like a virgin. "To go back to your original question…"

"Yes." Why on earth had she allowed into her bed a man she did not love before they were married? Come to that, why on earth had a woman like her accepted Gilbert's hand?

"Sir Gilbert offered for my hand, but he…he gave his offer with a condition." Philip could tell she was finding it difficult to say the words out loud. There was no need. He had already understood.

"He wanted to bed you first," he finished for her.

Whether this was to assert his authority over her

from the start, ascertain her willingness—and skill—in the marital bed, or simply to indulge his senses with a beautiful woman, he wasn't sure. What was certain was that it was the work of a perverted mind.

Philip made a grimace of disgust. Would there be no end to the man's depravity? God knew he did not expect much from his stepbrother, but pressuring a woman into sex was even worse than he would have given him credit for.

He remembered Rose's rigid acceptance when he had taken her into his arms, the way she had not made a single move toward him, said barely more than two words. She had been there against her will; it was obvious now. How had he not seen it? So convinced had he been that she was Lady Hershey playing hard to get that he had missed all the signs.

"Why did you accept this humiliating demand?" he asked, appalled. It was the first time he had made love to a woman who had come to his bed not in desire but because she felt she had no choice, and it did not feel good. That he had not been the one to force her into it did nothing to ease the guilt.

She bit her lip. "I know you must think me shamefully immoral for allowing a man to come to my bed before marriage, but…"

"I think nothing of the sort. In this instance the charge of shameful immorality needs to be laid at my dear stepbrother's door. He was the one who pressured you into accepting something you did not want. Therefore he, not you, is the one of whom a good opinion is irremediably lost to me. Not that it was particularly high to begin with, I have to say."

The fierceness in Philip's voice startled Rose.

Evidently there was no love lost between the two men, and he seemed more than ready to believe the worst of his kinsman, but still she was taken aback by his reaction. He was exonerating her of all blame, even though she had agreed to do something most people would consider the height of immorality, and he even seemed outraged on her behalf.

"Why did you accept such a humiliating proposition if you truly do not love Gilbert?" Philip repeated. He simply could not let it go.

"I told you I did not love him. It is no lie."

The words had darted out of her mouth. He nodded, relieved if not surprised. He could not imagine any woman harboring such feelings toward a man like Gilbert, much less a woman as delightful as Rose.

"So why did you allow him—or rather me—to make love to you?" He would have expected her to send to hell any man approaching her with such an insulting marriage offer.

"Do you really want to know?" Rose asked in a breath. How could he push her thus? Didn't he see how uncomfortable this conversation was for her?

"Let us assume I do want to know, since I asked the question. Twice."

The smile he gave her would have looked arrogant on anyone else, but on him it was almost endearing. He had calmed, since his initial show of temper, and she found herself breathing more easily. Formidable as he was, he would not harm her.

"I'm a widow. I have no choice but to remarry," she said simply. "My husband died in battle last year, and I have no means of subsistence. He was defending King Henry, and of course as we now know…"

Philip interrupted her with a raised hand. Indeed, now everything was clear. The man had chosen the wrong side and was considered a traitor to the man who was now King Edward IV. As a consequence, his allowance had been denied his widow. She was not the only woman in the country to find herself in this unjust situation right now.

"Have you no family to help you? No one who could intercede on your behalf to the king?"

Rose regarded him stonily. "Yes, I do. That is why I accepted your stepbrother's outrageous proposition. I enjoy being humiliated."

"There is no need for such sarcasm," Philip growled, impressed by her pique. Lord, but the woman had guts!

"Isn't there?" Rose hissed. What did he take her for? A weak-minded simpleton? Did he really think she would have allowed Sir Gilbert to demand her surrender if she had other options? "You said you wanted answers to your questions. I am merely complying with your wishes. It is hardly my fault if your questions are inane," she replied as scathingly as she had ever spoken to anyone.

An elegant eyebrow arched.

"Well, lady. I imagine you never dared tell Gilbert that *his* questions were inane, though it will not have escaped your notice that more often than not that is exactly what they are." Philip spoke quietly when she had expected him to flare up in anger at the provocation. "Because if he had seen just how fiery you are, he would never have made you any offer of marriage, even an insulting one, this much I can promise you. Gilbert is not man enough to enjoy being challenged, much less by a woman."

Rose could well believe that, but she had the odd impression that *he* was impressed by her defiance, rather than offended.

"Whether he would have enjoyed being married to me is neither here nor there, as he has made it clear he never wants to see me again."

Philip looked at Rose a long moment but could not bring himself to offer his commiserations. However bitter she felt now, she was better off well away from his stepbrother. Soon she would realize it.

"What do you suppose to do now?" he asked gently.

"I don't know. Why are you even asking?"

"I am only trying to help you."

"Help!" Rose let out a reluctant laugh. "You have an odd conception of help, my lord. Without you, Sir Gilbert would never have retracted his offer of marriage."

"Are you telling me that you regret it? That you would have gone through with it, despite the terms of his offer, despite the fact that you are not in love with him?"

She shrugged to mask the anguish this question provoked in her.

Love… She had found love in her first marriage, but she knew this was not the norm. She could not pretend to be so lucky as to find a husband who loved her a second time. Left to her own devices, now that Henry was dead, she would have preferred to remain unmarried, but she was not free to choose. Remarrying was her only way to get Edward back, and she would do much worse for him than wed a man she did not love.

So yes, with a bleeding heart, she would have married Sir Gilbert, on whatever terms.

"Why not? I don't have the luxury of choice. I need

a husband, and one man is as good as the next," she told Philip.

He frowned. "I'm not sure that is quite true. I'm not even sure you believe it. How would you like it if I said the same of women?"

"I would not like it," she admitted easily. "But perhaps you do think thus, since you did not realize that the lover you were holding in your arms last night was not the one you expected. It seems to me that one woman *is* very much the same as the next, as far as you are concerned."

"I did not hold you in my arms. I made love to you," he said in a purr. "More than once. I did not have time to think overmuch."

At the words, Rose went scarlet. There was no need to remind her of what he had done. She remembered it too well. "All the more reason to make sure that the woman in your bed is the one you want, don't you think?"

He was not so easily chastened.

"What I am trying to say is that we did not talk. You barely said two words to me and it was pitch dark. I think I could be forgiven for not knowing how a woman I do not know would respond under my touch," he argued with the same maddening logic he had displayed the evening before. "How was I supposed to guess that you were not Lady Hershey? Anyone else would have thrown me out of bed, and rightly so."

"It can happen! It *did* happen. I was not the woman you thought I was, and yet I did not kick you out!" she snapped.

"No, you most certainly did not." Philip's appreciative murmur sent her cheeks a deeper shade of red. His eyes had caught alight, and she could tell he would remember their night together for the rest of his life.

As would she, if for slightly different reasons.

"Please!" she whimpered. "I beg of you, do not mention what happened again."

"Not mentioning it will not make it disappear, just as talking about it will not cause further harm," he pointed out matter-of-factly.

Mayhap, but in the circumstances, Rose thought he was awfully nonchalant. He had just ruined her prospects of marriage, and even if, admittedly, the match would not have been one based on love or even respect, she would have thought he'd feel some sort of remorse over his actions.

Evidently Philip was not a man plagued by an over-zealous conscience or moral values. His argument that he could not have recognized her because he didn't know anything about his intended lover was quite shocking.

"And just so you know, I do not think that any woman is as good as another," he added, crossing his arms over his chest. "You are the perfect illustration of this."

Rose stared at him with wide eyes. What on earth did that mean? All she knew was that the conversation was slipping into dangerous territory. Philip's expression had become almost predatory. She had to get out of there before she became the prey.

Now that she had established she had gone to Sir Gilbert not in lust but because she had no other choice, there was little point in prolonging the moment.

"I told you I have been asked to leave. I fail to see why we are having this discussion."

His eyes clouded over. The burning intent in them was replaced by something resembling contrition. Oh. Perhaps he could be made to feel some guilt for his actions after all.

"Mayhap what I am trying to do is say that I am sorry."

She gave a scoff. "Are you really? If you were truly sorry, you would have gone to your brother and explained the misunderstanding by now."

"Stepbrother," he corrected automatically, as if the distinction was vital in his mind. "But I will not speak to Gilbert, as hearing that I was the one making love to you when he meant to have you for himself would not appease his anger. On the contrary. Even supposing he believed me, it would only make him more vindictive. He and I have never really got on."

No. Evidently not. His eyes had gone icy with disapproval, his voice hard, the way it did every time Sir Gilbert was mentioned. It wasn't difficult to guess that his hatred for his stepbrother was the reason he could not bear to be called his brother.

"So it is better to let him think I introduced a lover to my bed when I had already arranged to…meet with him?" she asked, incensed by the suggestion that her pride mattered less than the petty feud between the two men.

"If it is going to make him forget about his plans of marrying you, then yes," Philip said bluntly. "Haven't you got the measure of the man by now? Do you really want to be married to a man who thinks he can exploit your misery to satisfy his urges?"

This unexpected show of support failed to impress her. "What do you know about what I want, or need? We are strangers. We do not know each other!"

The words died on her lips at the thoroughly indecent look Philip threw her.

"We may not know each other, but I would argue that we are hardly strangers," he said, taking a step closer to her. "Strangers do not know the taste of each other's skin, do they?"

Rose gasped at the audacity of the comment. She had pleaded not to be reminded of their night together, barely a moment ago, and here he was, hinting that he had kissed every inch of her body and she had welcomed him inside of hers. Indeed, this was hardly a claim strangers could make, but she was not prepared to discuss it, now or ever.

"What did your conquest think of your defection?" she asked with a small, sarcastic smile. "I can imagine she was not best pleased to be supplanted by another woman."

"She was furious about having been refused entry to the castle, so needless to say I never even mentioned how I actually spent the night," he answered, superbly unruffled. "She upbraided me this morning for not honoring my word, so I cannot imagine her reaction if she had been told I had bedded another woman. Not to worry. I shall simply have to make it up to her later."

Rose gulped. Was he determined to put her ill-at-ease? He had just said he was sorry, but all he could do was place lewd images in her head. Lady Hershey was going to share Philip's bed tonight, and he was going to do everything he could to ensure that she got over her disappointment. If what she had seen last night was anything to go by, the woman would certainly leave the castle thoroughly satisfied. Imagining them in bed together made her insides flare up in an emotion she was at pains to identify. Then it struck her.

Jealousy.

It was not disgust or anger, it was jealousy, she realized with a measure of shock.

"Thank you for informing me of your forthcoming activities," she said with as much disdain as she could muster. "I hope you do not intend to seek me out tomorrow to apprise me of your exploits."

Philip tilted his head at the sharpness in her voice. He looked genuinely taken aback, as if he had expected her to enjoy the manner of his answer. She did not. "Forgive me if I have offended you, but I have never met anyone like you. You speak straight, and I thought you would appreciate the reciprocity."

"Well, I do not! I am honest, whereas you are just plain crude."

"Oh, dear, I have been accused of many things but never that."

"Please do not tempt me to add my own contribution to the list of all the things you have been accused of," she said dampeningly. "It would be all too easy."

His beautiful mouth quivered. "I do not doubt it."

"Now if you will excuse me, I will take my leave. I have delayed long enough."

To her intense annoyance, he did not let her go but instead followed her to the stables. Her irritation grew. When would he leave her alone?

"Is this your horse?" Philip asked, eyeing up the sorry palfrey. It had seen better days, or rather, many previous years.

"Yes," Rose answered crisply, understanding all too well what he had not dared say. "I cannot afford a new one." She stroked the mare's neck and lowered her eyes in embarrassment. The horse had been with her for as long as she could remember, and she loved it, but she should not have to ride such an ancient mount. Unfortunately, it was the only one she had left, and she wasn't even sure she would be able to replace it when it died. Her situation had never appeared more desperate than now, when she had lost all hope of marrying Sir Gilbert.

"I was not criticizing," Philip told Rose gently, seeing her pinch her lips like someone trying to keep tears at bay.

She had not lied. Evidently, she was not a rich woman.

Suddenly he understood her position a bit better. For all his faults, Gilbert would be an attractive prospect for a widow without protection and means. His fortune was by no means contemptible. It only made the terms of his offer more nauseating. To play on the vulnerability of a woman to extract an agreement from her was despicable. His ever-present contempt for the man boiled under the surface, threatening to erupt. His stepbrother had thought to exploit Rose's distress for his pleasure.

Had he married her as was intended, he would have made sure she felt in his debt all her life. He would not have allowed her to ever forget what she owed him. Once they were married, Gilbert would effectively own her, at least that was how he would see it. For him a wife was a commodity, nothing more. He would never love her, or even treat her with respect. He would simply exert his authority over someone he considered his property, someone who owed him obedience.

In the bedroom, it would have been even worse.

Gilbert had a cruel streak in him, and he would have enjoyed taming his reluctant wife and watching her fight her aversion for him, taken pleasure in knowing she was required by law to accept his touch.

His guts contracted in loathing. How could he be related to a man like this?

Then his irritation increased another notch when he saw that no one was getting ready to leave with Rose. Gilbert had not deemed it fit to provide an escort for a woman—a woman he had once promised marriage to, no less—or bothered to come and say good bye to her.

"Are you travelling alone?"

"I suppose I am. Unless you see something I don't," Rose answered, lifting herself into the saddle like a woman used to taking care of herself. She had not called for the groom or asked for his help. "Good bye, my lord."

Before he could say anything, she kicked her palfrey, which responded more readily than he had expected. A moment later, Lady Rose Maltravers had vanished through the main gate.

It only took Philip one heartbeat to make his decision.

Chapter 3

Judging by the fierce pounding of hooves, the rider coming up the road behind her was mounted on a younger, much fitter horse, and he was in a hurry. Rose nudged her mare to one side, giving him the opportunity to overtake her without slowing too much.

He never did.

A moment later Lord Chrystenden drew up by her side, astride a horse whose dark brown coat gleamed as much as his velvety eyes. Inexplicably, her heartbeat increased. Or perhaps there was nothing inexplicable about it. How could she not be affected by this man? Not only was he magnificent, the figure of the perfect knight, but only the night before he had made mad, passionate love to her.

It was difficult to get past that fact when she looked at him. He had done to her what only her husband had previously done and made her body explode in an unprecedented way in the process.

“Lady Rose.” He tilted his head.

“Have I forgotten anything?” she asked with a frown. It was unlikely. She had gone to Harleith Castle with nothing more than the clothes on her back and the few personal items in the saddlebags. But why would Philip set off after her in such an impetuous manner if not to return something to her?

“Not that I am aware of,” he confirmed with a smile.

What was he doing here, then? She looked around her. The forest was only a small distance away. Perhaps that was where he was heading. “Are you going hunting?”

“No. At least I do not *think* that’s what I’m doing.” This enigmatic answer made her arch an eyebrow. “I am here to escort you home,” he offered when he saw her confusion.

“Did Sir Gilbert send you?”

He gave a snort. “No. The man doesn’t know I’m here. I doubt he knows you have gone, or even cares.”

Even though she knew it wasn’t aimed at her, Rose flinched at the aggression in Philip’s voice. He’d just called his stepbrother “the man.” Why did he harbor such a deep hatred for him? Every time Sir Gilbert was mentioned, his stepbrother became a different person.

“Why are you here?” she asked instead of dwelling on the subject further. Any disagreement between them had nothing to do with her, and she had enough problems of her own to contend with.

“I could not bear the idea of you being on the road on your own,” Philip answered. “It is not safe.”

No, it probably wasn’t, but Sir Gilbert had not let this bother him. She marveled at the difference between the two men. The one who had once wanted to marry her had sent her away in disgrace without even enquiring as to her means of transport, while the one who had only met her by mistake was taking it upon himself to see her safely home when he surely had other things to do.

“Very well,” she said, kicking the mare onward. If he wanted to ensure her protection, she was not going to refuse. The idea of going through the dense woods all by herself was all she had been able to think about for the last few miles. An intimidating escort to keep danger at bay was exactly what she needed right now. "But what about the poor Lady Hershey? I thought you had plans regarding her tonight. Do not tell me you are going to disappoint her a second time?"

With a start Philip realized that he had forgotten all about Lady Hershey.

"Do you live far away?" he enquired, frowning. If it took the whole day to get to Rose's home, he would never be back at Harleith Castle in time to meet with the lady. He had not thought about that or anything else when he had so rashly set out after her. All he had known was that he could not bear the idea of her being alone on the road and out of his sight.

This was most unusual. Philip had always prided himself on his ability to think things through with a clear head and not rush into decisions. What was it about Rose that had made him do something so unlike him?

"I live just on the other side of the valley," she informed him lightly. "We should get there some time after *sext*."

"Then I should have time to gallop back home and honor my promise to Lady Hershey. Fret not. She will not miss out a second time."

"I hope not," Rose said with what she meant as heavy sarcasm. To her dismay it came out more like ill-placed possessiveness.

"Is this truly what you are hoping for?" he asked with one of his roguish smiles.

Damn. So he had heard the hostility in her voice.

This man truly was like no other. There was an unsettling depth of knowledge in his brown eyes. It was as if he understood things about her that she could not even apprehend. And why was she jealous of the woman? She certainly had no reason to be—she and Philip were nothing to each other. He had come into her life by mistake, and he would be out of it before the sun was down.

"Please make sure you do get to the castle on time. I would hate to be the cause of Lady Hershey's disappointment a second time."

He laughed. "She might have been disappointed, but I will own that I was not. I cannot imagine her or anyone giving me more pleasure than you did."

"I… This is not…" Rose was so shocked that he should dare say something like this to her face that she choked on the words.

"Come. You can admit it. You must be thankful that I came to your bed instead of Gilbert."

She stared at him. Of course she was, but she would never acknowledge such a thing. "If you think for a moment that I will answer that, you are sadly deluded!" She snorted.

"Not to worry. Your refusal to admit it is an answer in itself."

There was no mistaking the smile on his face. He was enjoying himself. Rose mentally berated herself. She should not have allowed him to rile her so. If he meant to unsettle her, she would never be able to compete with him. The man was a consummate seducer and far too disconcerting for her to stand a chance.

For the remainder of the journey, she stared purposefully at the road ahead and made a point of answering only his most innocuous questions.

Having encountered no incident on the way, they reached her house well before *none*, just as she had predicted. Dismounting, Rose felt a fresh burst of embarrassment, knowing that Philip would see in one glance the conditions she was reduced to. He had assessed her horse earlier on, in the courtyard at Harleith Castle. He would not miss the size of the modest manor or the state it was in.

"I thank you for your escort," she said to put an end to his scrutiny. Whatever she thought of him or his motivations, undeniably, it had been good to feel safe on the road. No one would have thought of bothering a woman under the protection of a man like Philip.

He waved the words aside as if he had done no more than what was expected of him, then regarded her fixedly. There was a strangely earnest look in his eyes, making the irises swirl like clouds of dust gathering before a storm. She had a feeling he was about to ask her something very personal, and she braced herself for what was to come.

"Your first husband. Did you love him?"

Rose froze in incredulity. This was even worse than she had feared. How dare he even consider broaching that topic? And how was she supposed to respond to such breathtaking impudence?

"What makes you think you can be so forward as to ask me this question?" she exclaimed.

The brown eyes never wavered. "The knowledge that you were ready to take Gilbert as your second husband, all the while feeling nothing but contempt for him. I cannot help but wonder if your first marriage was also one you did not desire."

The idea that she might have been married off against her will by unscrupulous parents sat uncomfortably with Philip. Was Rose destined to go from man to man without ever being allowed a say in her destiny? Unfortunately, it was the lot of more than one young woman.

Was she one of them?

But she raised her chin, the gesture telling him that, mercifully, no, she wasn't. From the way her eyes misted over, he understood that her first marriage had been a love match and that she missed her husband dearly.

He mentally kicked himself for rekindling what had obviously been a traumatic loss.

"I loved Henry, my husband," Rose said, stirred into defiance by Philip's brazenness. If he wanted to know about her personal life, then she would tell him the whole heartbreaking truth. "And he loved me, even though I was not as well born as he was. That is why his family never agreed to the match. I was not good enough, in Baron Chichester's mind. His son should have married an heiress to further the family's prestige, not offered his hand to the first girl he fell in love with. But Henry went against his father's counsel, and we…"

Her voice broke. Despite her intention to make Philip feel callous for reawakening the pain of her loss, she was the one suffering. She averted her gaze, unable to bear the look in his eyes. Not that it was harsh. On the contrary, it was full of compassion. But somehow his sympathy was more difficult to handle than his jibes would have been. It was as if he truly understood what she had gone through.

The sincerity and the depth of Rose's grief hit Philip hard—harder than he had anticipated. There was something in the way she refused to meet his eye that reminded him of himself, of how he tried not to crumble whenever he thought of his little girl.

He knew what it was to try and ignore the pain gnawing at your entrails when you thought of a loved one you would never see again, how difficult it was to look at someone and see on their face an empathy you did not want, an understanding which only made you feel exposed and all the more vulnerable.

Yes, unfortunately he understood all too well the way Rose felt right now, and his heart went out to her.

"If you and your husband loved each other, don't you think you owe it to him to marry a man who treats you like he would have done, instead of a rogue like Gilbert, who only wanted to take advantage of you? A man who discarded you without even hearing your explanations when you had done nothing wrong?" he asked gently. "What do you think Henry would feel to see you treated with such disrespect?"

The question was so eerily close to what she had been thinking that Rose gave a gasp. How had he guessed that she spent her days constantly asking herself what Henry would think or say? It was her way of fooling herself that he had not quite left her, that he was still somehow with her, a shadow by her side, helping her to survive his death and the loss of Edward.

It was as if Philip had read her mind, as if he knew she needed this presence, however illusory, in her life. Being understood so well did something to her and made her see this man in a new light. The soft voice and the understanding in his eyes were her undoing. Up until that moment he had been mocking, arrogant, infuriatingly smug, and she had dealt with it, because it did not really affect her emotionally.

But this last comment cut her to the quick because he was right.

Henry would have died a thousand deaths rather than see her reduced to accepting a man's insulting offer. If he had been told that she would be forced to sell her body to be reunited with the son his father had taken from her, he would have ripped the man apart with his own hands. But Henry was gone, no one was here to defend her, and her body was her only weapon. She would use it if it killed her, as it was the only way she could get her son back.

Her eyes filled with tears. She swiftly turned away to hide them, determined not to fall apart in front of Philip. Mercifully, he did not say a word or attempt to touch her.

After a long while, she turned around.

"Of course he would hate to see what I am reduced to, but what choice do I have?" she answered, doing her best to remain calm. "I have no place to call my own, no money. At least your brother took an interest in me, even if it was for the wrong reasons."

"Gilbert would never have…"

She cut him short, regretting having opened up to him. What use would it do to discuss all this now? She should have treated his questions with the contempt they deserved, not allowed the unexpected insight they betrayed to get to her.

Right now she wanted to be alone and curl up in a ball.

"I do not see what else we have to say to each other. You kindly offered to escort me back home, and you did," she said stiffly, knowing she was about to collapse in misery. "I thank you and bid you good day, my lord."

Unable to countenance another moment of this painful conversation, Rose made her way to the house, then stopped in her tracks. There was one last thing she needed to ask Philip before he left for good. Now was her chance. There would not be another. She returned to him slowly. His mouth twitched when he saw her retrace her steps, as if he thought she could not stay away from him. This arrogance would normally have elicited a stringent retort, but she bit it back.

It was not the moment to antagonize him.

She needed him on her side.

"There is something I would ask of you," she said, conscious she was throwing her fate into his hands.

"Of course," he answered with a slight bow.

"I would be grateful if you kept silent about last night's events. I would hate for everyone to think me a…to know that I accepted…to, well, to take me for what I am not." By the time she had finished she was stammering dreadfully.

"Please, my lady," Philip said with a raised hand. He was no longer smiling, and her heart lifted in hope. Mayhap he would agree to the request after all. "I swear on my honor that no one is going to find out about it through me. Only you and I will ever know what happened in that bed and why. But…"

"But?" Her heart plummeted. She should have guessed it would not be that easy.

"I'm afraid I cannot vouch for my stepbrother's discretion. He might well delight in the retelling of the story."

Rose gave a whimper. She hadn't thought of that. Of course Sir Gilbert would not let her get away with humiliating him thus! He would make sure he got his revenge. That he did not know the identity of her supposed lover would not protect her from slander. What mattered was that she had taken a man to her bed. Who that man was hardly made any difference.

Philip remained silent for a moment, considering. There had to be a way out of this tangle. He could not bear to have Gilbert drag Rose's name through the mud for what was, ultimately, his mistake.

"He might not boast about it if I make him see that it would only be humiliating for him. Gilbert has always been very mindful of appearances. I will make him understand that he has more to lose by spreading word of your indiscretion than by keeping silent. No one knew about this betrothal, you say. It shall remain a secret," he stated, plunging his gaze into hers. "I will convince him that people will cast doubts about his skills as a lover if they get wind of what happened. They will automatically assume you had thought him incapable of satisfying you in bed and had made sure to find a man who could while you still had the chance."

Rose flushed when she remembered how utterly she had come undone in his arms. Yes. She had certainly been satisfied.

"Do you think it will work?"

"I will make sure it does." His tone brooked no refusal, and her shoulders sagged in relief. If anyone could convince Sir Gilbert to stay silent, it was his assured stepbrother.

"Why are you agreeing to help me so easily?" she murmured.

"Why did you ask me to help you if you didn't think I would accept?" Philip countered, moved by the genuine gratefulness in her eyes. Truly this woman was irresistible. And even if she hadn't been, how could he not agree to help her when he was the cause of her predicament?

"I thought I had to at least try, but I didn't dare hope you would want to help me."

"Then I am happy to surprise you." He smiled. "I have more honor than to boast about an adventure that could have serious repercussions for a lady."

"Thank you." Rose did not even think of doubting his sense of honor. Hadn't he insisted on escorting her when it hadn't been his responsibility?

"I went to your bed by mistake. I cannot change that, so there is little use in bemoaning the fact. In doing so, I ruined your prospects of marrying Gilbert. I can live with the idea because I know I did not bed you by evil design and because I genuinely believe that you are better off away from my stepbrother." Philip spoke through clenched teeth, betraying the animosity she was well aware of by now. "But if I now reveled in the situation and exposed your mistake for all to laugh at, I would be a poor excuse of a man, don't you think?

This extraordinary declaration surprised her so much she didn't even think about lying. "Well, if I'm honest, I…"

"Please, don't be!" Philip laughed, saving her from further embarrassment. "I can see what you are thinking all too clearly. You felt the need to ask me to keep silent about what happened, so you cannot have thought me capable of much delicacy."

"No, I didn't," she admitted boldly.

There was no point in lying. She *had* been angry with him. She had felt so duped, so cheated out of the solution she had found to remedy her pressing problem, that naturally she had laid the blame at his door. But now she had calmed down, she could see Philip had done nothing wrong.

It had, as he'd said, all been an unfortunate mistake.

How could he have imagined that the woman who was lying in his bed, who did not seem surprised to feel a man's hands on her body, who had allowed him to make love to her not just once but twice, would not be the woman he had agreed to meet? And even though he could have washed his hands of the whole adventure and spared himself the trouble of escorting her back home, he had ridden with her. He had apologized to her, after a fashion, and he was now telling her he would be careful not to endanger her reputation.

It was more than she could have hoped for.

Although she suspected his unusually protective attitude had a lot to do with the dislike he felt for his stepbrother, she could not help but congratulate herself on the fairness of his dealings with her.

"I will not keep you any longer, my lord," she said with a small smile. "I believe you have a pressing arrangement for tonight."

Philip stared at her blankly for a moment, then cursed under his breath.

Christ, once again he had forgotten all about Lady Hershey.

****

Later that night, as he stared at the ceiling, Philip mused on the day's events.

Despite a busy love life, he had never made love to a woman by mistake before. He usually relied on seduction or sheer brazenness to lure his conquests into his bed. He had even been known to use deceit on occasion, but he had never gone to anyone by mistake.

Next to him Lady Hershey gave a sigh. He had made

it back to the castle in time to bed her after all. Now she was asleep, sated by their lovemaking, but he was strangely restless. The encounter had not afforded him half the pleasure he had promised himself. She had pursued him with a rare and very promising eagerness, and he should have relished possessing her, but the odd adventure with Rose kept playing on his mind, leaving no room for anything or anyone else.

Try as he may, he just could not forget her.

Perhaps it was little wonder that she should fill his thoughts. Had he not so unexpectedly decided to come back to Harleith Castle after his sojourn in London, she would have been bedded by his stepbrother, the man he despised the most on this earth. The idea was enough to make his blood boil.

Thank God he had been the one losing himself inside her delicious flesh, not Gilbert.

Just thinking of their night together set his senses on fire, something Lady Hershey's actual caresses had failed to do earlier. He had felt oddly detached during the whole of the proceedings, not that she had noticed anything was amiss. Her moans of pleasure had made it clear that she was more than satisfied. By morning, though, he knew he would want her to leave and never come back again. Even before they had kissed, a dalliance with her had lost all its piquancy, courtesy of Lady Rose, who had burst into his life in so shocking a manner.

He resolved to have a word with his stepbrother at the earliest opportunity and find out more about the lady he had almost married. To think she could have become his sister-in-law! Had Gilbert not walked in on them as he had done, the wedding would in all probability have gone ahead as planned.

Philip tried to imagine his reaction if he had waked in the morning to find a stranger nestled in his arms instead of the woman lying next to him right now. He would have thought he was going mad. Then he pictured Rose opening her eyes at sunrise and seeing him in bed in place of Gilbert. Would she have been horrified? Relieved? Aroused?

Would she have slapped him?

Remembering the sharp sting on his cheek, he smiled to himself. No other woman had been able to get away with doing such a thing. Many had tried, but he had always been fast enough or, more to the point, awake enough, to stop them. A bubble of incredulous laughter rose inside of him. How much more fiery could the woman get? One thing was for sure—she would have made a terrible bride to his dull, pompous stepbrother. He would never have been able to handle such a spirited wife.

Perhaps he should have allowed the wedding to go ahead after all, since Rose had been so distraught to see the betrothal broken. It would prove good entertainment to watch Gilbert try to deal with a woman like her. He could always speak to him, explain that it had been a misunderstanding and convince him to marry her anyway. After all, what Rose and Gilbert did with their lives was no business of his. If they were both bent on this enormously mismatched union, who was he to deny them? They were responsible adults.

But then he imagined Gilbert taking Rose to bed, and his whole body heaved in protest. He knew he would not lift a finger to save the marriage. The idea of her going to his stepbrother's bed night after night and having to endure his touch, when she had only married him to save herself from poverty, was unbearable. It left no doubt in his mind that she did not desire him any more than she loved him. Her attitude the previous night had made that clear.

Now that he knew the circumstances behind their lovemaking, everything made sense.

At first he had been surprised by her diffidence and lack of enthusiasm. But of course the lover in his arms had not been Lady Hershey, the seductress who had thrown herself at him so boldly. It had been Rose, a woman who did not want to be there. She had thought him to be Gilbert, a man who was forcing her hand most shamefully, so he could understand why she would not want to encourage him any more than necessary.

With his caresses, Philip had soon made her inhibitions melt, but still she had not said a word, nor had she accepted his embrace when he had wanted to draw her into his arms afterward. At the time, he had been too spent to give it more than a passing thought, but now he remembered the way she had tensed up as soon as he had tried to cuddle up to her.

Rose had allowed him to possess her but not to show her any proof of tenderness. She had given the man she thought to be her future husband access to her body because she'd had no choice, but not to her soul. She had refused him any intimacy afterward, and kept her emotions to herself. Perhaps she had felt guilty for experiencing pleasure in the arms of a man she despised, or perhaps she had resented the fact that she had melted in the arms of someone who was not the husband she had loved.

This more than anything else told him that he should

do everything in his power to stop Gilbert from marrying Rose. He did not deserve a woman like her.

But now this wedding would never happen.

So why was he so upset about the whole affair? He should be relieved. After all, nothing irreparable had happened, and Gilbert had not taken her against her will. It wasn't the first time he had seen his stepbrother do something he disagreed with. Usually his outrage did not last for long. Over the years he had become quite adept at pushing Gilbert's antics out of his mind, but this time he had the impression he would never forgive him for this villainy.

He gave a sigh and concluded that, however involved he was now, he would forget about this adventure with Rose soon enough. His infatuation for a woman had never outlived their lovemaking. The only exception to this had been Hettie. But he had been young then, untried. She had been his first conquest, and of course, she had borne him a child… It was little wonder he should have found it hard to let her go.

Why should Rose be any different to the dozens of women he had made love to since? True, with her the lovemaking had preceded their actual meeting, but he did not doubt that before the week was over the beautiful lady would have vanished from his mind. As would Lady Hershey. If he was honest with himself, he had taken her more to repair the wrong he had unwittingly caused her than through actual desire.

What was wrong with him? Bedding one woman by mistake and not being able to forget about her, and taking another one whilst knowing all the while that he did not really want to?

He had to get a grip on himself.

"Philip?"

A voice reached his ear, a hand landed on his shoulder. He had subconsciously turned his back on Lady Hershey while he was thinking about Rose. The message was pretty clear, but of course she was unaware of the direction his mind had gone. He kept still, hoping to discourage her.

"Philip? Are you awake?"

The hand carried on its exploration onto his front and then lower down. He clenched his jaw. How was he going to get out of another bout of lovemaking without hurting Lady Hershey's feelings? It was not her fault his mind was full of another woman, and he did not want to disappoint her, but he would not be able to indulge her a second time.

He simply didn't want to.

"I'm tired," he growled, doing his best to give the impression that she had wakened him.

"Don't worry, you won't even have to move," she whispered in his ear, before forcing him onto his back. He had to stop her now, or it would be too late.

"Please. Not now."

She never answered. Philip's eyes closed, and he understood that he would have to indulge her a second time after all, only not in the way he had imagined. Perhaps it was for the best, he reflected. He could not afford to let Rose Maltravers take over his life.

Soon he stopped thinking altogether.

Later that morning, he left Harleith Castle with no intention of coming back.

Chapter 4

Waves crashed ashore and seagulls cried overhead, but Rose could not see anything. The mist around her was impenetrable, eerie, just what she needed to calm her shattered nerves. She pushed on, relishing the sting of the sea spray against her skin, the bite of the cold wind on her face. Had she stayed a moment more in the accursed litter, she feared she would have suffocated.

The groom travelling with her had tried to dissuade her from going to the beach.

"My lady, you cannot go, it's too dangerous," he had cried. "One cannot see more than a yard ahead!"

"I do not need to see. I just need to be alone."

Without another word she had gone in the direction of the beach, the image of Edward's distraught face haunting her mind. It had been only the second time she had seen him since Henry's father had taken him so cruelly from her. He had changed so much in two months! Soon he would be one year old. Her son was no longer a babe, he had become a beautiful little boy.

And she had missed it all.

She had not been there to see him take his first steps or hear his first words, someone else had had the privilege of seeing it all. He was now walking, even if at times he was still unstable on his feet, and his vocabulary had come on remarkably well. A clever, precocious boy, the image of his father in every way… When she arrived, he had looked at her with big blue eyes that were so much like Henry's that she had been unable to talk for a long, long while, unable to do anything except keep him in a tight embrace.

How long would it be until she saw him again? He was so young, still. Would he forget her? Would he one day speak to her, his own mother, as he would to a stranger? The longer he stayed with Baron Chichester, the more distant their relationship would become. In all probability Henry's father was already trying to steer him away from her, the woman he had deemed so unsuitable to raise his grandson. The last few months had been hell without Edward, and the thought that she could lose him forever wrenched a desperate sob out of her, a raw, almost animalistic sound.

She fell to her knees, hugging herself.

****

A curlew or a seagull, perhaps, Philip wasn't sure. In any case the chilling sound reached to the bottom of his soul. Was the animal mortally wounded? He looked around, in vain. In this fog he could not have seen a galloping horse until it was about to run him over.

He pressed on.

The walk was not particularly pleasant, what with it being so cold, but it was better than being confined to the smoky great hall with his cousin and his dull wife for yet another day. He cursed himself for having been persuaded to pay them a visit. He should have suspected it would be as dreary as it always was. The man was a frightening vision of what Gilbert would be in ten years' time, self-important and obnoxious.

As soon as he got back to the castle, Philip vowed, he would make up a pressing engagement and take his leave. Perhaps he would go abroad for a while, to clear his mind.

Months had passed since his encounter with Rose and, much to his surprise and annoyance, he had not been able to get her out of his thoughts. Every time he saw a horse he wondered if she had replaced her old mare yet, when he saw a piece of jewelry he automatically pictured her wearing it, and he found it impossible to see a lady in a blue mantle anywhere without going to her to ascertain her identity.

Why had he been unable to push her out of his mind? This inability to forget a woman was unlike him. Since he had been obliged to give Hettie up he had not felt any attachment for anyone.

Today he was feeling quite weary. He had spent the last few months hearing people congratulating him on his title earned on the battlefield fighting for King Edward. These people he did not know took it upon themselves to tell him that Sir Thomas would be proud of him for becoming a lord. But as true as that was, he knew that such a distinction would not have mattered overmuch to his stepfather .

He would have been more interested in seeing the man he had become.

Titles, land, and fortune were not what he had judged a man's character on, and he had tried to impress upon his children from a young age that a happy family life was more important than all the possessions in the world. Alone amongst his peers he had not condemned Philip for wanting to acknowledge the daughter he had fathered onto a simple maid. On the contrary, he had been proud to see him take his responsibilities and stand by the woman he had got with child, young as he had been.

But in the end, it had been Hettie herself who had put an end to their affair. Even if he understood her reasons for doing so, he could not deny a pang of regret at the idea that they had never been able to build a family together. Though she had not been of suitable birth, he knew he would have been happy with a woman as selfless and loving as Hettie and the children she would have given him.

The people who patted him on the back since he had been made Lord Chrystenden had no idea that what Philip hankered for was not recognition from the king but a fulfilling family life. Having seen firsthand how difficult relationships could make one's life hell, he craved serenity.

He braced his body against the wind and gave a sigh.

Serenity… With a brother like Gilbert, he was as likely to get it as he was to turn into a griffin.

****

Rose stood, brushed the sand from her knees, and walked on. How far had she walked? How long had she been gone? Where was the litter? She had no idea, but she was not worried. The ethereal world around her was like a balm to her bruised soul. It was as if nothing was real, and for a moment she could fool herself that all would be well, that her son was waiting for her at home, that she would be able to scoop him up into her arms and tuck him into bed herself tonight.

A silhouette materialized slowly ahead of her, at first nothing more than a shadow in the mist, then unmistakably a person, walking in her direction. A man. It seemed that, contrary to what she had hoped, she was not alone on the beach. Another few steps and the breath caught in her throat… Henry? He'd come back to her! She shook her head, berating herself for her folly. Of course it was not him, he was dead! How long before she stopped seeing him everywhere she went, or rather hoping that it *was* him? Still, the figure was familiar.

As it moved closer, her heartbeat increased in foreboding. This particular way of moving could only belong to one man.

The man who had haunted her every thought for twelve long weeks, the other man she thought she saw everywhere she went. She came to a halt, determined to flee before he could recognize her, but her feet refused to obey her.

She had not moved an inch when he finally stopped in front of her.

"You here!" she breathed, incredulity making her blink.

"I could say the same to you," Philip answered in the mocking manner she remembered so well. "Or I could greet you in a more conventional, polite manner. Good day, my lady." He bowed with all the civility she had failed to show him.

But Rose was too stunned to feel guilty. She could not believe she was seeing his dark hazel eyes appraising her so impudently, that she was hearing his voice teasing her in velvety tones, and she could not believe that her body was reacting in such a way to these eyes, to this voice, to this man she had tried so hard to forget.

As soon as he appeared in front of her she understood that it had all been a vain hope. She would never forget Philip, Lord Chrystenden. For one, they had made love. How could a woman ever forget a man who had taken possession of her body in such a breathtaking manner? For another, he was just too fascinating, just as arresting as he had been three months ago.

His hair was longer, the look in his eyes even fiercer.

Her cheeks flushed, her heartbeat went wild, her breath became ragged.

It was unseemly, unsettling.

"Do you enjoy being outside at the mercy of the elements, my lady?" he asked her with a smile. "It is not exactly a pleasant day for a walk on the beach."

"No, but I…I needed the fresh air," she stammered. "What are you doing here if you think the day is so unpleasant?"

"I suppose I was in need of fresh air too. I am visiting my cousin and his wife up on Rorland Manor and cursing myself for the impulse. Sleet and thunder would be preferable to a conversation with them, so I am more than happy to contend with wind and fog. All the more so that it afforded me a meeting with you."

Indeed, he seemed pleased to see her, which surprised her. She had half expected him to need to be reminded who she was if they ever met again.

She blinked, unable to quite believe they were having this conversation. The fog surrounding them made everything unreal, and Philip more like an imaginary being than a man of flesh and bones, almost a vision come as an answer to her problems. Only a moment ago she had been wondering what to do, and he had appeared out of nowhere, almost literally, as if to provide her with an answer. But what answer?

Then she remembered what he had told her during their argument at Harleith Castle.

If there is anything I can do to help, I will do it.

Well… There was one thing he could do.

"You would have to marry me," she said, speaking slowly, as if in a daze. Being married to a powerful man would indeed solve all the problems in her life.

"Marry you?"

Philip tilted his head in amazement. Rose and he had not set eye on each other for nigh on three months, not since the night he had made love to her by mistake and then seen her safely home the next day. Neither of them had imagined they would ever meet again after they parted, and now she was asking him to marry her? For a moment he thought he had misheard her, with the wind howling about them. But perhaps he had not. For there was one reason why she would ask for his support.

He stilled.

"You mean… Are you expecting my child?"

It was possible, of course. They had definitely slept together, twice, and he had not even tried to be careful. As he had imagined her to be Lady Hershey at the time, he had assumed she would have taken her precautions against an unwanted pregnancy, drinking potions and visiting wise women to ensure her numerous dalliances did not bear fruit.

But Rose…Rose would not have been prepared. She was not a seasoned temptress. She did not need to guard herself. If anything, she might have taken some herbs to facilitate conception before her meeting with Gilbert, thinking that if she fell with child that night it would only strengthen her position. She had been set on marrying him, regardless of her feelings toward him, and if his stepbrother had been crude enough to demand his marital rights before their actual wedding, she might have thought to make the best of a bad bargain by trapping him before he could change his mind.

And he could not blame her.

Gilbert was as slippery as an eel. Anyone with any sense would want to bind him to his word.

Still. *He* had not set out to trap her. And he was now being told that he had fathered a child onto the woman he had bedded by mistake! He shook his head, not knowing if he should be appalled or amused. Not since he was eighteen had he been caught out thus.

"Your child," Rose said in the same slow, dreamy voice.

He could not decide if she was ashamed at finding herself with child, as unmarried women were sure to be judged harshly for it, or just plain shocked to walk into him before she had summoned the courage to go and find him. Her eyes were sparkling with unshed tears. Had she been crying, not knowing how to solve her dilemma, or was this merely a result of the sharp wind sweeping the beach? No wonder she had needed fresh air—she had just found out she was pregnant from their unintended encounter.

He remembered the cry of anguish he had heard earlier. Not a wounded animal, then, but a woman in distress, genuine distress. He could not count this as a ploy to make him feel guilty, or sway his decision, as she had been unaware of his presence on the beach at the time.

No, her torment was all too real. He could see plainly that she was not feeling well. Her eyes were red rimmed, and her soft features had hardened.

"Would you really marry me if I was carrying your child?" she murmured, her eyes strangely vacant. She seemed prey to a dream.

Philip gave a mental curse, but there was only one

answer to this question. He could not be a rogue who did not face his responsibilities toward a woman he had bedded, even if he had not meant to cause her any harm. Barely a moment before he had walked into Rose he had been thinking that he wanted to make his stepfather proud. Well, here was his chance.

It was not difficult to guess what Sir Thomas would have expected him to do in the circumstances.

"Of course I would. Unless you had already found yourself another husband?" he asked. Considering her desperate financial situation it was possible that she would have thought to remedy the problem as soon as she could.

"No, you are the only man I've slept with since my…" Her voice wavered. "You are only the second man who…"

"I understand," he cut in with decision. This was not what he had asked, but he understood all too well what she was saying. Even if she had been betrothed to another man, there could be no doubt about the identity of the baby's father. She had not been bedded by anyone else, and he believed her.

That settled it. If she was really pregnant with his child, he would not let another man marry her and take it away from him.

Philip took a deep breath. Unlikely as it was, he was about to propose to a woman he had never thought to see again. If someone had told him when he got up that morning that he would be engaged before the end of the day, he would have thanked him for providing him the first opportunity to laugh since he had entered Rorland Castle.

"Consider us betrothed, my lady," he said, before

taking her hand in his. "Your troubles are at an end. We shall be married before the end of the month." In other words, before her pregnancy started to show. She would not have to face public disapproval alone. "I will arrange everything. In a few days' time I will send an escort to bring you to Wicklow Castle, my new residence."

He kissed the tip of her fingers and turned on his heels before she could protest. He had once allowed Hettie to talk him into not marrying her, and he was not about to let Rose do the same. This time he would do what was right and look after his child properly.

As if in a dream, Rose watched Philip disappear into the mist. His words were floating in her mind.

Consider us betrothed.

She nodded to herself, unable to fully apprehend the enormity of the situation. Lord Chrystenden was going to marry her. In a remote corner of her mind she knew that the consideration should stir some sort of emotion within her, but her whole body had gone numb, and her brain was as foggy as the beach around her.

"My lady? Where are you?"

Another silhouette appeared behind her. The groom! She had quite forgotten about the faithful old man. When he insisted, she followed him back to the litter. She did so without a word, feeling as dizzy as if someone had just hit her on the head.

Once she was back at home, in her familiar environment instead of surrounded by eerie fog, some sense returned to her, and Rose understood the full magnitude of what had just happened.

She had just agreed to marry a man who thought her pregnant with his child.

How could she have let such a thing happen?

She retraced her steps to the front door. It was not too late to go and find Philip to rectify the situation. Rorland Manor could not be too far, if he had walked from there to the beach. She had to go to him and set things straight. Even if marrying a man like Lord Chrystenden was the answer to all her prayers, she knew she could not go through with it. She could not lie. She would have to tell him the truth. She was not carrying his heir, she was not in love with him, and even if she had been, she did not want to get married to him under such false pretense.

What would Henry say? A fundamentally honest person, he would have been horrified at the deception, and rightly so.

Of course all the blame did not lie at her door. She had not actively lied, she had never even said she was pregnant. Philip had somehow convinced himself on his own that she was, and she had said nothing to the contrary, too dazed to think straight. Her mind had been too focused on Edward and her fears of losing him for good, and the fog had not helped. It was as if the whole scene had happened to another person.

Still, she should have pulled herself together before she agreed to marry him!

With a jolt Rose realized that she hadn't agreed to marry him, either. He had simply assumed that she had. Disbelief made her blink. Philip had once made love to her by mistake. As a consequence of this night together she had unwittingly led him to believe that she was pregnant with his child and had given her tacit agreement to a proposal she had neither sought nor desired.

What a mess!

If she did not speak out now, by the end of the month

it would be too late. Philip was not a man to prevaricate or to allow anyone to stand in his way once he had taken a decision. Before she had time to breathe she would be married to a man she did not know and who…

Who was wealthy and powerful enough to get Edward back for her.

Rose stilled, while everything came into focus.

He had said that his title was new. She remembered Sir Gilbert saying that his stepbrother was a staunch supporter of the king and had been from the onset. To be made a lord he would have earned his sovereign's gratitude on the battlefield, and been one of his closest allies.

No one, least of all Baron Chichester, who would be well-advised not to draw attention to his past Lancastrian connections, would dare go against the wishes of such a man. What little she had seen of Philip had shown her how daunting he could be in his anger, and if he really had the ear of the king…

Hope surged through her. With Lord Chrystenden's support and his wealth at her disposal, it would not be long before Baron Chichester relented and handed Edward back to her. If she married him, she would get to see her son grow up after all.

Rose raised her chin. As soon as the idea that she could get her son back entered her head, she could not get rid of it, and she knew she would go ahead with this marriage. Of course there would be an uncomfortable confrontation when Philip discovered he had been duped. The idea of facing his wrath was enough to make her rethink the whole thing. What punishment would he dream up to make her pay for the dreadful lie? He did not seem like a vindictive man, but when he talked about his stepbrother you could see a steely core under his soft manners. Was it wise to take such a man for a fool?

After he realized he had been manipulated, there was no telling what his reaction might be.

It mattered not.

Even if he made her pay for the rest of her life, she would not be worse off than she was now. Nothing frightened her as much as losing her son did. She would endure anything not to let that happen. She had once been prepared to let Sir Gilbert use her body. Marrying Philip seemed small sacrifice by comparison. It was not as if she had a choice. She could not spend the rest of her life knowing she had not jumped at the chance to get her son back.

Philip had indeed provided her with the perfect solution to her problem.

She closed the door and decided she would wait for events to unfold.

Chapter 5

Rose was pale, and her face was drawn. It was the first thing Philip noticed when she arrived at Wicklow Castle. It had been the case that day on the beach as well, but the mist had somehow made it less glaring. Now, in the sunlight, it was all he could see. She was nervous as well, and seemed to have lost weight. This did not surprise him. She would have been racked with anxiety about her future and that of the illegitimate child growing inside her. He could well imagine her shock upon finding out their mistake had resulted in an unwanted and highly compromising pregnancy.

It might also be that her pregnancy was difficult, like Hettie's had been. The first few months had been hard on her. He remembered how she had been sick every morning for weeks on end, and nauseous for the rest of the day, making her unable to eat as much as she should have. Mayhap Rose was suffering from the same misfortune. Whatever it was, she certainly was not the picture of blooming health people usually associated with pregnant ladies.

It only comforted him in the knowledge that he was doing the right thing by marrying her, precipitated and unplanned as the decision had been. He could not let a woman waste away in worry over her future when he had the means and, more importantly, the responsibility to put an end to her torment.

Not to mention that the idea of never seeing his child grow up tore at his chest. If by some miracle Rose managed to find a husband after this blow to her reputation, he might not prove to be a stepfather as generous and kind as his own had been. He could not let his child be raised by someone who did not love it as it deserved.

Fathers were supposed to be there for their children, and he would make sure he was.

It was not just a question of honor. He *wanted* to be there for this child in a way he had not been allowed to be for Emma. He wanted to be the father Sir Thomas had been for him.

And he wanted its mother, undoubtedly. Rose Maltravers stirred his senses and piqued his curiosity all at once. It was not a bad start for a marriage.

"My lady, welcome to Wicklow Castle, soon to be your residence," he said, kissing the tip of her fingers. "Worry not. Your problems are at an end. You are not alone any more. I will take my responsibility in this affair."

Contrary to what he had hoped for, she paled even further. Far from being reassured, she looked about to be sick. The babe, and not his words, were responsible for it, he told himself.

Rose could barely suppress a wave of nausea upon hearing Philip's words of reassurance. Her future was *not* his responsibility, she had only arranged it that way for her benefit. She was deceiving him shamefully—he had no idea he was being used for the status a marriage with him would bring her.

The thought of her treachery made her insides curdle.

But looking at Philip's steady gaze she knew he was right in at least one thing. Her problems were about to end. As Lady Chrystenden she would have power. She would no longer be a defenseless widow Baron Chichester could override. Indeed she was not alone anymore, and her future husband was a man to be reckoned with, an important courtier with access to the king himself.

This man would get Edward back for her, even if at the moment he had no idea of the mission she entrusted to him. Trepidation made her stomach flip. How on earth was she going to broach the delicate topic, and when?

My lord, now that we are married, would you come with me and get my son from his grandfather's custody? The baron might very well make a fuss, perhaps even turn physically violent, and you will have to stand up to him on my behalf. I know I never mentioned I had a child already, but I didn't think it was important. Do you want to go and get Edward now or wait until we have actually consummated our marriage? The sooner the better, as far as I'm concerned, but by all means, please finish your cup of ale first.

The prospect was a frightening one because of course telling him about Edward would not be the only terrible revelation she had to make.

May I take this opportunity to inform you that I am not carrying your child after all, and never was? I only went along with the pretense to make the most of your position. Shameful of me, I know, but we are married now, so there is nothing you can do about it. Would you care for another wafer?

Straightening her spine, Rose forced a smile. "Thank you, my lord. I am grateful."

"We are betrothed now. Please call me Philip. I shall call you Rose."

She could not do that, not yet at least. Rose promised herself to only use his name when she had revealed the truth behind her reasons for marrying him and heard that he had forgiven her for the deceit, if that day ever came.

She remained silent, and the corner of his lip curled up. He had not missed her refusal to even acknowledge the request, but mercifully he did not seem put out by her reaction.

"We are to be married the day after tomorrow, if it pleases you. It is rather sudden, but in the circumstances, I'm sure you will agree it is for the best," he said, offering her his arm.

She accepted it, determined to behave as the perfect wife until she revealed just how completely she had taken advantage of him.

"It does suit me, thank you."

If it were up to her, they would be married right now and bound for her father-in-law's estate before dusk.

In the great hall, a fire was roaring in a hearth big enough to accommodate whole tree trunks. The floor was strewn with rushes and sweet-smelling herbs, the numerous seats covered with embroidered cushions to make them more comfortable and sheepskins to ward off the cold. Though the newly made lord had not lived here long, he had evidently lost little time in tailoring the castle to suit his tastes. This room was the most welcoming one she had ever been in, the house of a man attentive to his and his guests' comfort and pleasure.

"How do you like your new home, Rose?" he asked her pleasantly, pouring spiced wine into a cup.

The use of her name, as well as the reminder that she

would soon be his wife, made her blush. Fortunately his eyes were focused on the task at hand and she was afforded some time to regain her composure.

"Very well, thank you."

"And your new horse?"

"She is the prettiest and best-behaved mare I have ever ridden," Rose enthused. She had been surprised to receive the gift a few days after meeting with Philip on the beach. He had sent her a palfrey to her stables, along with a message that an escort of four men at arms would be bringing her to Wicklow Castle the following day. The future Lady Chrystenden was to travel in style and under close guard.

"I am glad. I knew you two would suit as soon as I saw her," Philip said, plunging a red-hot poker into the wine to heat it.

Indeed, the mare would be a suitable replacement for the sorry palfrey she was used to riding. The unusual golden color of her coat reminded him of Rose's hair. The way it had draped over her shoulders the night he had wakened to find her glaring at him from the side of the bed had fascinated him. It had flowed and shimmered every time she moved, as if it had a life of its own. The elegant horse would be the perfect match for its rider's graceful mien, and the two together would make for a striking pair.

They were meant to be together, just like the sun was meant to shine over verdant hills.

"What will you call her?" he asked, replacing the poker in the fire.

"Emerald, I think."

Philip's eyes sparkled in amusement. "Emeralds are green," he said with a twitch of his lips. "Have you seen your horse?"

Rose flushed a delicious pink. "I know that Goldie or Sunshine would perhaps be a more apt name for her, but… Emeralds are my favorite gems, and she came with a green caparison, the color of which reminded me of the stone. Of course, if you prefer me to give her another name, I will."

"You do not have to justify your choice of name, Rose. She is your horse, not mine," he said, raising his hand. "Ours is not going to be the kind of marriage where you have to seek my approval in every aspect of your life. You need not fear I mean to control your every decision. I trust your judgment."

"You…you do?"

She sounded so taken aback that he wondered if he had not been too hasty. She sounded like someone who had steeled herself for a fight and found out when she was about to throw a punch that her opponent actually wanted to shake her hand. But why would she be so afraid of being opposed?

"Are you telling me I should not trust you?" he enquired, arching an eyebrow.

"No, of course not," Rose answered hurriedly. Heavens, this was getting too close for comfort. Another moment and she would blurt out the truth, that she was not pregnant with his child. "I am gratified to hear that I will be free to make my own decisions. So Emerald it shall be," she said instead, choosing to revert to the safe topic at hand.

"Be careful. The mare has quite a temper on her, for all she appears well-behaved. That is why I knew you would be well-suited, you are both full of spirit under a distractingly beautiful exterior," he said in what sounded suspiciously like a purr. “I would watch her, if I were you. At any moment she might bolt.”

Philip handed her the steaming cup, a flame lurking in his eyes. Rose knew he was thinking of the time she had slapped him, but oddly, he did not seem disapproving.

“I am sure she will bristle if provoked, as most animals do, so I will be sure not to do anything to displease her,” she said, taking a sip of wine to hide her confusion.

“Very wise.” There was laughter in his voice, and she knew she would see warmth in his eyes if she dared to look at him. She did not.

She could not allow herself to get a glimpse of a thoughtful, funny, caring man or she would not be able to go on with the deception. It was one thing using an unscrupulous rogue such as Sir Gilbert for her selfish purpose, quite another to play the same trick on an unsuspecting, honorable man trying to do his duty by her, and she was starting to suspect that Philip was a warm-hearted, worthy man who did not deserve to be treated so callously.

Once her anger had abated, on the morning after their encounter, she had been forced to re-evaluate her opinion of him. His had been a genuine mistake, and he was not the only culprit. She’d had her share of blame in this affair. He had done his best to atone for it and even compensate for his stepbrother’s less than gentlemanly treatment of her, escorting her back home and offering his protection. He had been generous and helpful when he had nothing to gain from it.

What she had seen of him since that day had only come to confirm this first impression. Anyone spending time with Philip would quickly come to the inevitable conclusion.

He was a good man.

He was doing his best to repair the wrong he had inadvertently caused her. They did not have to marry—he could have offered her some money for the raising of his bastard child, and even that would have been more than what most men would have been expected to do. But Philip had proposed without the least hesitation, and instead of appraising him of his mistake she had jumped at the chance of becoming his wife, all the while knowing she was taking advantage of his generosity. Rose would never have described herself as a selfish person before, but perhaps she was.

No.

Selfish was not the word, for she was not doing this for herself. She was doing it all for Edward. He deserved to be raised by his mother, his mother who loved him, not by a man as cold and calculating as Baron Chichester, who would only force her loving, happy little boy into a replica of himself. If there had been any way to ensure she could get her son back without deceiving Philip, she would never have used him so.

But there wasn't.

She emptied the cup with decision. The dice were cast.

"My lord, you called?" a blonde girl entered the room, providing a welcome distraction.

"Yes. Rose, this is Emeline," Philip said, gesturing to her to come forward. "She will be your lady-in-waiting."

"My lady." Smiling as if she was delighted to make her acquaintance, the girl swept her a deep curtsey.

"This is kind of you, but I do not need…" Rose started.

Philip interrupted her with a raised hand. Before he said a word he dismissed the girl and everyone else present. Rose's heartbeat instantly went wild. Was he about to remonstrate with her? He had just said theirs would not be the kind of marriage where she had to seek his approval in every way, and yet he did not seem disposed to have his orders questioned.

"Have you brought any lady-in-waiting with you?" he asked once they were alone.

"No, for I do not have any."

"As I thought. Then Emeline will be your lady-in-waiting."

"You said earlier that I would not have to refer to you for every aspect of my life," Rose reminded him.

"I did, and I mean it. But this is different. You seem to think that I should not have gone to further expense on your account, and you feel guilty that I hired people to see to your comfort. You feel as if you are an unwelcome imposition."

"I…" Rose bit her lip. She had thought precisely that, but she would not admit as much.

"Let me assure you that you are nothing of the sort. A wife is not an imposition, and providing you with what you need is not only my duty but also my pleasure." He looked at her squarely, and she saw that he meant every word. "Please do not go against my wishes in this, Rose. I will not have you living in less than the comfort you have been accustomed to."

Rose barely repressed a snort of incredulity. From what she had seen so far, as mistress of Wicklow Castle she would be treated in a way she had *never* been accustomed to. Because of Baron Chichester's disapproval at their union, she and Henry had not been able to afford a life of luxury.

She had not minded, as their modest income had been enough to see to their needs and those of the elderly couple who served them, but still she had often wished they could stop having to worry about the price of every little thing they bought.

Seeing she remained silent, Philip pressed his advantage.

"Besides, I'm afraid that Emeline will take it very personally to be dismissed. She is a gentle soul, and she was over-awed at the idea of becoming Lady Chrystenden's lady-in-waiting. Being told now that she is not, after all, going to attend to the lady of the castle would be a crushing blow to her. You wouldn't want to have that on your conscience, would you?"

"Oh, you are cruel, my lord!" Rose breathed. "Playing on my sensibilities thus."

"I know. Unbearably cruel."

To Philip's relief a smile bloomed on Rose's lips, transforming her face. For the first time since she had passed the castle gate she looked happy. His own lips curled. It felt good to be the cause of her happiness, and he suddenly wished he had been there to witness the pleasure on her face upon receiving Emerald.

"Very well," she said, tilting her head. "I see that I have no choice but to comply."

****

Philip opened the door for Rose, then took a step back to let her through.

"This will be your room. I hope you find it to your satisfaction."

“I do, thank you.”

Indeed it would have been difficult to be dissatisfied. The room was just as welcoming as the great hall was, and showcased the same attention to detail. It was a very feminine room, light and airy. Had he had it furnished especially for her, she wondered?

“Please do not read anything into the fact that the tapestry depicts a scene in which Philip the Apostle plays a prominent role,” he laughed, glancing at the wall opposite her. “It was there when I bought the castle. I did not want to remove it, as it keeps the draughts out, but we can have it replaced by one more suited to your tastes later on.”

This answered her question. Of course he had not gone to the trouble of having a room made for her! A week ago he’d not even known he would get married…

“Worry not. I have very simple tastes,” she assured him. “My own bedchamber is nowhere near as grand as this one.”

Philip cleared his throat. He had not missed the way Rose kept taking nervous glances at the bed behind him. She did not even seem to realize she was doing it, but he did not want her to feel ill at ease.

“Rose. I will not bed you until we are married,” he said, forcing himself to ignore what his body was telling him. He could have taken her right now if she had expressed the wish. “I do not want you to think that I…” He stopped.

The last thing he wanted was for her to think him as dishonorable as his stepbrother and demand his marital rights before they were husband and wife. Damnation! How long would the memory of the wretched man stand between them? It was bad enough that he had to contend with the ghost of her late husband. Was it too much to ask that she thought of him without constantly comparing him to other men?

"I thank you. Yes, I…I think I would prefer to wait until we are married," Rose murmured.

Unlike before, she had a choice. Her agreement to be bedded was not the condition to a union between them. Though the idea of Philip taking her to bed did not make her heart flutter in dread like the prospect of enduring Sir Gilbert's attentions had, she could not prevent a deep sense of relief because she was not sure what her reaction would be once she lay in his arms.

This time when she went to his bed, it would be in good conscience, and it would be pleasurable. What had happened in Harleith Castle made that clear. How would she deal with it? Pleasure had taken her by surprise the first time. She had been unable to fight it, and she had not chosen to be there. After so long without a man, her body had surrendered to her lover's caresses regardless of what her mind was telling her.

But now…

Now it would feel like a betrayal to Henry.

Would she fight Philip despite the pleasure he gave her, unable to accept how he was making her feel? Would she allow herself to revel in it at the risk of feeling guilty afterward? Neither option seemed like a good option.

It was better to wait until it was absolutely unavoidable to make love to him. Perhaps she should even wait until she had revealed everything before going to his bed. That way she might feel less like she was shamelessly exploiting him for her own benefit.

Besides, once she was naked he might see that her

body had not changed in the least and start questioning her supposed pregnancy. He had not seen her naked that night at Harleith Castle, but he had touched her, and she had no doubt he would recall every inch of her body, just as she did his.

"Of course. I understand," he said slowly. "We will wait."

He pierced her with a look few men could have managed without appearing threatening. It made her whole body catch ablaze. His words were saying that he could wait, but the dark intent in his eyes belied the promise. His control was hanging by a thread. At the least encouragement he would tumble her into bed. So why was she resisting the temptation to do so? Did she really want to deny herself the pleasure she knew he could give her? Mayhap if she allowed him her favors and gave him access to the body he desired she would feel less wretched for the trick she was playing on him. In his arms for a brief, blissful moment she would forget everything that was not his kisses, and she would stop thinking, stop worrying about what she was doing…

And then… Then it would be worse. She would be racked by guilt and remorse, ashamed of herself for using her body thus. Besides, she was certain Philip wanted her to come to him because she desired him, not for any other reason, not as some sort of reward for behaving honorably toward her. If he suspected she had opened her arms to him to thank him for proposing to her, he would be horrified, and rightly so.

"Thank you. Yes. I think it would be better to wait."

"I will leave you to get settled, then. Good night, Rose."

"Good night, my lord."

"Philip," he reminded her softly.

"I can't," she breathed. "Forgive me."

"Of course. Soon."

Once the door was closed she fell onto the bed before her legs could give way from under her. She had been at Wicklow Castle for less than a day and already her nerves were reduced to shreds.

****

In the morning they broke their fasts together. The pleasure of sharing a meal with someone who was both attentive to her comfort and interested in what she had to say was indescribable, and Rose allowed herself to enjoy this comparatively harmless delight to the full. Mornings had been her favorite time with Henry. They would spend time together, laugh, and exchange heated kisses, before each going to their activities.

Mayhap it would become a favored moment with Philip too?

Comforted by the thought, she helped herself to a hearty serving of gruel. Now that she was here, so much closer to achieving her goal, her appetite had returned. In the last week, worried that Philip might have forgotten all about her in the arms of a beautiful temptress as determined as Lady Hershey or decided to go back on his promise to marry a stranger, she had barely been able to eat a thing.

Today, tempted by the delicious food served at Wicklow Castle, she made up for lost time.

"Do you always have as much of an appetite in the morning?" Philip enquired, watching Rose help herself to a piece of fruit from the dish opposite her. She had just finished her bowl of gruel and had cut herself a slice of venison pie.

"I… Yes, I do, I'm afraid," she stammered, dropping the pear she had taken.

"Worry not. I was not accusing you of being a glutton." Philip laughed, seeing her contrite expression. "I was wondering, that's all. Women in the beginning of their pregnancy sometimes have a delicate stomach in the mornings, but thankfully you don't seem to be suffering from any discomfort."

Oh, God. For a moment Rose had forgotten all about the babe she was supposed to be carrying.

"Indeed, I am not in the least affected. Please, do not worry. I am told that the women in my family experience little inconvenience while they carry their babes," she lied. In actual fact she had been sick for most of her first pregnancy, but of course she could hardly tell him that. Besides, she had to explain why she did not seem to suffer.

"I'm glad. I would hate to see you in pain on account of my child." He gave her a smile and picked up the pear she had discarded. "Here. Shall I peel it for you?"

"There is no need."

"No," he agreed, before throwing her a wicked smile. "Indulge me."

Something fell to the bottom of Rose's stomach.

She could not do this. She could not lie to a man like Philip. He was too thoughtful, he treated her too well. With Sir Gilbert she had never suffered a moment's remorse over her actions, but now… Now it was different. The man she meant to use for her own benefit was not a lecherous swine but an honorable man attentive to her needs.

Not only was she marrying him only so she could use his power and influence to her own ends, but she had given him hope for a child. She could tell he was looking forward to becoming a father. Right now the way he had said those words, "my child"... There had been so much pride in his voice, so much hope in his eyes! He wanted the babe, and finding out it had never existed would be a crushing blow.

It wasn't fair. She knew all too well what it felt like to hanker after a child and feel the loss of it deep in your bones. Could she really be responsible for another person's pain? She would be no better than Baron Chichester if she made Philip go through such trauma.

Maybe it was not too late. Maybe if she told him now, before they got married, that she had been mistaken, that she was not pregnant after all, that she had misread the signs, he would be spared the worst of the pain. The longer she waited until she disabused him, the more he would start imagining a future as a father.

"There is something..." Rose started but the door opened on the steward before she could finish her sentence.

"My lord. Mistress Henrietta is here to see you."

In his surprise Philip dropped the pear, much as Rose had done earlier.

Hettie! What was she doing here? He had not thought he would see her before he got married.

He got up before Master Thorne could introduce her into the room. The last thing he needed was for her and Rose to meet before he'd had the chance to explain the situation to either of them. Hettie deserved to be told about his impending union, and he wasn't sure how Rose would handle the revelation. Many ladies would not take it too kindly to be told that their husband's former sweetheart, a woman of low birth who had given him a bastard child, was still welcome in his home as if it was hers.

Guilt sliced through him. It felt disloyal to keep a secret from the woman he was going to marry.

No, he reasoned. It was not so much a secret as a part of his past that should not affect her. He was not trying to hide something from Rose because he did not trust her, he was merely waiting for the right moment—and manner—to tell her. What had existed between him and Hettie could not be explained away in a few sentences, and he wanted to do both her and Emma justice.

"Will you excuse me, Rose?" he asked, kissing the tip of her fingers lightly. "I will see you tonight."

"Of course."

As she watched Philip go, Rose did not know whether to be relieved for the unexpected reprieve or put out that she had been denied the opportunity to do the right thing.

****

"I wish you and Lady Rose all the happiness in the world!"

Philip could not help a smile at this reaction he had fully expected. Hettie had always been of a generous disposition, and he had known she would be glad for him.

He did not mention the fact that Rose was carrying his child, however, as he did not want to reawaken the pain of their recent loss. He felt guilty to be looking forward to this new babe when Hettie was still finding it hard to cope with the loss of their little girl. It felt like a betrayal, even if deep down he knew it was not.

"As a matter of fact, I have news of my own. That is

why I came to see you. I am expecting a child." She blushed and placed her hand over her stomach. Now that her fingers were pressing on the fabric of her gown, he saw that it was slightly rounded already. A smile bloomed on his lips. "It will be born in about five months' time."

"Oh, Hettie!" He drew her into his arms and placed a gentle kiss on her forehead. This was the best news she could have had.

"Do you not…"

"No." He cut her short with another kiss to the temple. He was not jealous or thinking less of her for giving another man a child. She was happily married to a good man, and he wanted nothing more than for them to have a family together. "I am happy for you. Scott will be a good father for your son or daughter."

"Thank you. I wish Emma could have met this new babe," she said with a sigh.

"I know, sweetheart. Me too."

As he closed his eyes Philip did not see Rose slip into the shadows.

****

As she lay in bed that night, Rose pondered the significance of the scene she had witnessed in the morning.

After her copious meal, she had wandered off to the lists for much needed exercise and walked straight in on Philip and another woman locked in an intimate embrace. The way he had cradled her made it abundantly clear that she meant a great deal to him, even though it was obvious from her raiment that she was no noblewoman. He had been both protective and gentle with her, and she was sure she had heard him use the word "sweetheart" in a voice full of emotion.

To think that all this time she had worried about brazen, sophisticated seductresses trying to lure him into bed! Perhaps she should have realized that such women would never pose any real threat to her, as they would only appeal to his senses for a brief night of passion.

But this one, a sweet soul who commanded his affection rather than stirred his blood… She did not quite know what to make of her.

Would she be a rival for her husband's attentions?

And what did it matter if she was? She was not marrying Philip because she loved him, she reminded herself, but to get her son back, and if he found his pleasure with other women, then all the better. She was not here to be entertained in bed.

So why was she so restless, as if she expected the door to open any moment and reveal Philip's tall frame?

The tapestry hung over the far wall drew her eyes every time she moved. Another Philip… How ironic that she had been placed in a room dominated by Lord Chrystenden's namesake! But the man in the center of the tapestry was wizened and frail-looking, with a long gray beard, an image of pious devotion that stirred no emotion in her.

The man she imagined in his stead was strong and broad-shouldered, with sparkling dark eyes, the epitome of the virile man who could tumble women into bed at a moment's notice and make their senses catch aflame.

The thought that this body, these eyes, were promised to her was enough to make her heart beat uncontrollably. Soon they would be married. She would belong to him and he to her. Soon she would be able to stroke his long limbs and drown in his velvety gaze without guilt.

To her shame, after having been interrupted on the verge of a confession that morning, she had not found the opportunity or the courage to go to Philip and tell him she was not really with child. It would seem that she was a coward as well as a despicable schemer… Well, she would have to make her peace with that. As long as she could be a mother to her son, she would accept every sacrifice.

Things would proceed as planned. Tomorrow night Philip would sleep in that very bed with her and make her his wife. And perhaps before the end of the week she would be reunited with Edward.

Her life, interrupted for a cruel moment, would finally resume its course.

Chapter 6

"My lady, a word with you if I may…" Emeline whispered in Rose's ear.

"What is it?"

The girl's eyes flicked toward the other ladies helping with the wedding preparations, and Rose understood she preferred to speak without an audience. Sighing, she led her to a small room next to her bedchamber that seemed to serve as a sort of study but was mercifully empty. It was easier that way. She was still not accustomed to the fact that she could order so many people around, and she would have felt uncomfortable asking half a dozen women to leave the room for no reason.

"Well?"

"Pardon me, my lady, but I could not help noticing in your bed this morning…" The girl blushed, and Rose knew what she was going to say. Her heart plummeted.

"Yes. I know."

When she had wakened, all-too-familiar cramps had seized her. She had hoped to keep the matter secret, but evidently the girl had seen the spotted sheets. There would be no trying to hide the fact now. She made a face at the irony of the situation. Her courses had started today of all days, on the morning of her wedding to Philip. It was as if fate was having a good laugh at her expense.

"What will you do about your wedding night?" Emeline sounded aghast at the development. "His lordship will not be best pleased to learn that your monthly courses have started!"

"No, he will not," Rose agreed.

As Philip believed her to be with child, and that was the very reason he had proposed to her, he would not take it too well to be told he was unable to consummate their marriage because she was bleeding. Rose could see one grim way out of the mess. She could claim that the blood had another cause, that she was having a miscarriage. After all, it would solve her other problem. She was now supposedly three months pregnant, and yet her figure had not changed. As her stomach would remain flat in the weeks to come, it would not be long before Philip started to get suspicious.

Yes. Pretending she was losing the child was her only option to salvage the situation.

But the idea of feigning a miscarriage horrified her. As a mother of a healthy child she had been separated from, she could not bear to fake the loss of another one.

Suddenly the web of lies in which she had gotten herself entangled threatened to suffocate her. What was she to do?

Emeline, who had no idea her mistress was supposed to be pregnant, was not so easily upset. "My sister was faced with a similar problem on her wedding night," she volunteered candidly. "We could do what she did then and stem the flow of blood with a pad of sheep's wool during the ceremony. It worked for her, and allowed her groom to perform his marital duty afterward. If you removed it just before his lordship…"

Rose raised her hand in disgust. "Please. There

won't be any need for such stratagems."

"Indeed there won't."

The masculine drawl made both women shriek. Philip stood up from behind the fire screen, his face a dark cloud. Rose's body froze in horror. He had been there the whole time! He had heard everything and drawn the inevitable conclusion.

"I am not sure there will be a wedding night after all," he said in a low rumble.

"My lord!" Emeline fell into a curtsey. Somehow Rose managed to remain erect, fighting the weakness that made her want to collapse in a heap herself. Philip stared at her for a long, interminable moment.

"Would you please leave me and Lady Rose alone?" he asked the trembling girl. Rose barely repressed a whimper. Though his manner toward Emeline was pleasant, his eyes, for her alone, were flashing in fury.

Once the door was closed, Rose prepared herself to face the onslaught she was sure to come. It never did.

Instead of lashing out at her, Philip walked to the table and started to fidget with a quill he found there.

"Once, when I was twelve years of age, I overheard a conversation which was not destined for me," he started to explain calmly, his eyes on the goose feather in his hand. "What I heard that day spared me a lot of trouble later on and probably saved a dog's life."

Saved a dog's life?

This was the last thing Rose had expected him to say right now. He sounded lost in some distant memories, when they both knew he should be mad with anger after the discovery of her treachery.

"D...did you?" she stammered, utterly at a loss. Philip was eerily calm, too calm for someone who had just been told he'd been made a fool of. Could it be that he had not understood the significance of Emeline's words? It seemed too good to be true.

"Yes. My life would have turned out very different had I not so opportunely overheard what I did that day." His voice was level, uninterested almost. The quill rolled back and forth between his forefinger and thumb, the only movement in the room. "It is true what they say. Forewarned is definitely forearmed."

With a sinking heart Rose realized that although Philip's voice had not been raised, and the story had seemed disconnected at first, he was commenting on what had just happened.

"If you let me…"

"Explain?" he cut in just as softly. "There is no need. It is all perfectly clear. The only thing I am not quite sure about is how you intended to get yourself out of this tangle. I presume I would have been told some time in the next few days that you had unfortunately lost the baby you were carrying."

He placed the quill back onto the table before making his way to her. Rose watched on, transfixed, as he brought his hand to her face. First he cupped her cheek. Then he let a finger trace a path from her eye down to her chin. A corner of his mouth lifted in a grim imitation of the warm smiles he usually gave her. His expression was icy cold.

She swallowed hard.

"Tell me, Rose, would you have cried when you told me? Just how good are you at pretending? Quite good, I imagine. After all, you had me convinced you were pregnant. Would the loss of your dear child have wrenched tears from your eyes? Would you have cried?"

he repeated, his finger carrying on with the caress. "Fool that I am, I believe I would have comforted you and swallowed my own pain to console you."

He spoke in a low, forlorn voice. Rose could feel her legs wobbling. This contained anger, this sadness, was a hundred times worse to handle than an outburst of temper would have been. She had fully expected to face Philip's wrath. She would have understood him lashing out at her. But this?

This was nothing like what she had prepared herself for.

She had been right to suppose he wanted the child, and it was obvious that the pain of its loss had lacerated him.

The weight of the guilt she had been carrying around for days suddenly overpowered her.

"I'm sorry. I swear I did not mean to mislead you…" she started hurriedly. "It all happened so quickly. That day on the beach you asked if I was carrying your child, and I…"

He did not appear to have heard her and cut through her words without raising his voice. "Presumably in a few months' time you would have come to me and announced you were to give me a child after all, having made sure I serviced you until you fell pregnant."

Serviced. Rose winced at the horrible word. He lifted her chin, and she saw that his eyes were glittering with intent. The temper she had feared was finally about to explode.

Immediately she took a step back. He let her go, but watched her with increasing coldness.

"Or perhaps you are barren, who knows? Either way you would have got what you wanted from me, a prestigious title and money to spend."

"I don't care about that!" she cried, shaken out of her torpor by the unfair accusation. She had not been after his fortune or status, she had only wanted her son back. If it was true she had deceived him, at least it had not been for such frivolous, shallow reasons.

"Do you not? Am I to believe you unquestionably when you tried to trick me into marrying you after you narrowly missed getting my stepbrother? When I have seen for myself in what conditions you live? I know you need money, Rose. You told me so yourself. And I remembered it too late." The corner of his lips lifted in a sinister smile. "I should be flattered that my performance in bed should have prompted you to choose me as your next victim. You were not so bad yourself, lady, though not enough for me to overlook your treachery, I'm afraid."

The venom was piercing though the velvety voice now. Rose could see that Philip was about to lose control. He would never have spoken to her in such scathing terms had he not been beside himself with fury and disappointment.

"This is not…"

"One last thing," he interrupted again. "Did you plan to lie all along, or did I give you the idea myself when I asked you if you were pregnant with my child that day on the beach? Please tell me, so I know just how big a fool I am."

"It wasn't like that!" She wrung her hands in despair. "You are not a fool, and I…"

"Spare me your protests, my lady, I am not in the mood to hear them. My stepbrother escaped a lifetime as your husband. Now it is my turn. Congratulations on being the first person to make us feel equal." He gave an ironic bow. "Needless to say, now, the wedding is not going ahead. You will not have to endure your lady's unsavory ideas to stop nature from running its course. This should come as some consolation to you. I bid you good day. We need never meet again."

Philip left, marveling at the fact that he had managed to hold himself together. His fingers were itching to grab something, or someone, and he prayed that no one would cross his path right now for fear he might do something irreparable. Never had his control been in more danger of slipping.

What a sobering comedown!

For years he'd been chased by countless admirers and pressured toward marriage by his most determined conquests. Despite the constant solicitations, no one had ever tempted him into proposing. Rose was the only woman to whom he had offered his hand. And she had made a fool of him.

How unbearably humiliating!

He had done the honorable thing by her, and she had pounced, taking advantage of his unusual moment of weakness. This went to show that he should never have dropped his guard, even if she made him feel the hitherto unprecedented urge to be spontaneous. Only with her had he ever acted on impulse, only she had made him forego his usual caution. It had felt good, liberating even, not to ask himself so many questions and simply follow his instinct for once.

But look at the result!

The only solace was the fact that, as this wedding was to be a small affair, no one was here to witness his humiliation, least of all Gilbert. And thank God he had not told Hettie he was going to be a father.

Philip bunched his fists.

The revelation of Rose's duplicity had been most timely. Any moment now they would have been making their way to the chapel. The wedding was to take place before *terce*. Soon the priest would be searching the castle for the elusive bride and groom. Perhaps it was for the best that he had elected to celebrate this union as discreetly as possible, for this last-moment cancellation would have been the scandal of the year. He had not foregone the lavish celebrations befitting his new status because he was ashamed of Rose, despite her apparent lack of suitability for the role of Lady Chrystenden, but because she had been the one suggesting a small, private ceremony and he had thought to please her by agreeing to it.

At the time, he had attributed her decision to delicacy and a wish for discretion. This would be her second union, and the first had been a love match, so he understood she did not want people to draw comparison between the two men. He had also thought she was so relieved to be spared the indignity of being with child whilst unmarried that she had preferred security over pomp.

Of course now he knew otherwise.

She had simply been eager to secure his hand before he changed his mind about marrying her. A penniless widow was not the bride a man of his consequence should have chosen. He might have considered her as a mistress, but certainly not as the wife a newly made lord needed to start a prestigious family line.

Even more importantly, she'd had to secure the alliance before he started asking too many questions and found out her little secret.

Namely that she was not truly with child.

“Hell and damnation!” he swore out loud, and made his way to the stables, knowing he needed an outlet for his rage.

He remembered her small house, her aged horse, her plain clothes, and marveled that he had not taken into account just how desperate for money she was when she had accepted his offer to become his wife. But a woman reduced to such extremities as to agree to marry Gilbert despite the insulting terms of his offer would have thanked her lucky stars to be asked to become Lady Chrystenden. She would have jumped at the chance of marrying such an eligible party, a man both more powerful and more honorable than his stepbrother. All the clues had been there, so why had he been so blind?

As soon as the idea that she might be with child had crossed his mind, he had proposed to her, without any confirmation needed. Rose was right in at least one thing—it had all happened too quickly, and through his own fault. Despite his anger, he had the fairness to recognize that she had not been the one suggesting marriage to him. He had done that all on his own.

Why? What had made him rush into this marriage?

He stopped in his tracks when the answer struck him. Deep down he must have wanted to be married to Rose. It was the only explanation. Would he have offered his hand so readily if he had not secretly desired this union? Would he have arranged everything so swiftly and so efficiently if he had not been ready to marry her? No. He would have asked questions, found out more about her past, or at least waited a few days before announcing his decision to her.

Instead he had proposed and left immediately afterward, not even giving her the chance to reject him. How could he blame her for making the most of his unexpected offer? Any woman in her place would have done the same.

He had been the fool, not she.

She had made no secret of her desperate situation. Hell, she had once sought to wed Gilbert despite her feelings about him! If not for his fortune and title, why would a woman be bent on marrying a man she plainly despised? Having failed to secure one brother, she had jumped at the chance of securing the other. And he had handed her that chance on a silver platter. He had asked her—nay, *told* her—they were to marry, and had made it impossible for her to refuse.

He stormed into the stables and vaulted on top of his horse, not bothering with a saddle. He needed to do something to alleviate the tension building in his body. He could not remember ever being so angry—or rather, so disappointed with himself.

How could he have allowed himself to get into such a situation? To think he had wanted to protect Rose from the shock of meeting Hettie yesterday! He had felt guilty for keeping his past life a secret from her when he had done nothing wrong. What he had done before their marriage had nothing to do with her. There was no shame in it. Rose should have been the one ashamed of herself!

What had this woman reduced him to? Where was the level-headed man he'd thought himself to be?

Rose had played him like a lovestruck youth and a gullible fool, when he was neither. He should have known better. She had intended to use him as she had once thought to use Gilbert. How could he bear the idea that he had been as easily manipulated as his stepbrother, on whose advice he would not buy so much as a loaf of bread!

There was only one explanation for this uncharacteristic lapse in judgment. The memory of his night with Rose had perverted his mind, making him incapable of thinking straight. Hadn't he found it impossible to forget her, a most unusual development for him? Their eerie encounter on the beach, when the shock of seeing her after so long had quite floored him, had not helped. At the sight of her windswept hair and reddened cheeks, his body had given a jolt of recognition, something strong and impossible to ignore, almost like a punch to the gut.

And when she had said he had to marry her… By then he had already reached that conclusion. Marrying her would be the only way to stop obsessing about her.

Yes, that was the worst of it. Rose had not manipulated or forced him into anything. He had done so on his own, because of his inexplicable craving for her.

And all because of his stupid mistake! Had he not made love to her that night, had he not experienced so much pleasure in her arms, he would not have been so easily swayed. Of course she would not have been able to claim she was carrying his child if they had not shared a bed… Philip hated the fact that his urges had overruled his reason. He could bed as many women as he wanted, but the choice of a wife should not be left to his senses, and should have a sounder basis than desire.

But that was the crux of the matter.

That day on the beach he had suddenly understood that he did not want to make love to scores of women, he wanted only this one. He could not bear the idea that he would never make love to Rose ever again. And the only way this would happen was if he married her. She was not going to let him anywhere near her otherwise. As he had thought her pregnant with his child, both his urges and his honor would have been satisfied.

It had been the perfect solution.

Except…

Except that it had all been based on a lie! She was not carrying his child. He was not going to be a father or, more pointedly, it had never been a possibility. The fury sweeping through him when he had heard Emeline and Rose discuss her monthly courses had less to do with humiliation than with the crushing of his hopes.

Hearing that he was not going to be a father had made him realize how much he had wanted that child. Ever since the death of his little girl, even though she had never truly lived with him, there had been a void in his life, a void no one but another child would ever fill.

Philip kicked his horse into a heedless gallop, desperate to ease his pain, more desperate still to cool his heated senses.

He had left Rose abruptly for fear that his bitterness would lead him to behave dishonorably. For a moment, all he had thought about was making her pay for her deception, for the destruction of his hopes, to stretch her over the table, plunge inside her softness and ride her until he could not think. It would have been nothing more than she deserved. If she had thought to use her charms to manipulate him, then she should be prepared to face the consequences.

He shook his head in self-loathing.

What was he thinking? Rose had not tried to use her charms on him at any point, whether to placate his anger or to convince him to reconsider his decision not to marry her. There was no use trying to tell himself that as they had already slept together there would be little harm in it. Taking her to appease his anger would have been the act of a despicable coward, nothing more. She wouldn't have wanted him and would have willfully ignored the fact. Since when did he behave like this?

This woman really was messing with his mind and inflaming his desire in a shocking way.

Dressed in the gown he had chosen to flatter her voluptuous figure, she had been a vision, the most alluring bride he had ever seen. Would he ever manage to get the image out of his mind and forget about her?

He stopped the horse so abruptly that he caused it to rear up in protest. Not a chance in Hell. He had not been able to forget Rose when she had been nothing more than a woman he had bedded by mistake, so how would he forget about her now that he had thought to make her his wife, now that she had, briefly, in his mind, been the mother of his child?

Shadows were descending on the hills beyond. Night was closing in.

Had he not elected to go to the small room to gather his thoughts before the wedding, he would have been none the wiser about Rose's deception. She would be his wife by now. Unaware of her scheming, he would have married her as planned. A part of him wondered if it would not have been better that way. What you did not know could not hurt. He would be taking her to bed even now, unable to wait a moment longer before possessing her and making the union indissoluble, even though of course the consummation had already taken place.

By mistake.

As usual Philip felt himself harden at the memory of their night together, and he gave a loud series of curses. He would not be able to leave things as they were. He would have to go and find Rose before she left.

Chapter 7

Dazed, Rose stared at the quill on the table.

How could it have gone so spectacularly wrong?

When she had been told she would not marry Sir Gilbert, as depressing as the realization had been, on a personal level she had been relieved. The only benefit of a union with him would have been to get Edward back, and nothing else had seemed important, but she had not wanted him.

With Philip it was the opposite. The advantages of a marriage with him, though considerable, were nothing compared to the comfort brought to her by the idea of having him for her husband. She had never thought a second marriage would be anything other than a necessity, something she would have to endure if she wanted to live a decent life with her son, but she was forced to acknowledge that with Philip there might have been more to it. They might have laughed, teased each other, found pleasure in and out of bed, had a happy marriage.

In any case, it was all idle speculation now. She looked at her wedding dress pooling at her feet in a cascade of velvet. All this effort, all those lies for nothing…

What would she do now?

She picked up the quill and rolled it between her fingers like Philip had done earlier, pondering on her best course of action. Should she write him a note of apology before leaving, to explain the reasons behind her deceit? How would she word such a revelation? Would he even read it, or would the letter be thrown into the fire unopened? There was no way of knowing.

A tentative knock made her start.

"My lady?" Emeline's voice came through the wooden door.

"Come in," Rose answered wearily, placing the quill back on the table. She would never be able to write such an important letter in the state she was in right now, or possibly ever.

The door opened on the frightened girl. "Is his lordship gone?" she asked in a whisper that betrayed more terror than reverence.

"Yes, he is. You can help me out of this gown. It will not be required after all. There is to be no wedding."

"Oh, no, my lady! Was it something I said?"

Rose gave a snort. How did the girl imagine she had enough influence to put Lord Chrystenden's wedding in jeopardy? But when she saw genuine worry on the pale face in front of her, she did not have the heart to mock Emeline, even if she dearly needed to unleash her own bitterness.

"Don't worry," she soothed, leading the way back to her bedchamber. "It has more to do with something I did."

Mercifully, the room was empty. There would be no need to face her ladies' questions or looks of sympathy. Silently she turned her back to Emeline so she could unpin the headdress and start unlacing the gown. Suddenly she needed to be out of this sumptuous outfit. Philip had selected it, and it did not belong to the likes of her. It was a dress fit for the mighty Lady Chrystenden, a symbol of what she could have been, of everything she could have had.

The money that would have saved her from poverty, the support of a prestigious husband, the champion she needed to get Edward back, none of these would be hers now. Neither would the man she wanted.

Because, undeniably, she wanted Philip.

She had never thought such a thing would happen, and so soon after Henry's death, but it had. After a happy first marriage, she had never hoped to know the happiness of being married to a man she loved and admired a second time, but over the course of the last week she had come to see that perhaps Philip could one day be that man. His considerate behavior toward her had convinced her they could have grown to like and respect each other. Could they have one day come to feel even more?

She shook her head. It was no use wondering about such things now.

She let Emeline strip her of all her finery and, dressed once more in her old, plain linen gown, went to the garden, the garden that could have been hers.

Dusk had started to descend, blurring the edges of the horizon. Rose gave a sigh.

Had the wedding gone ahead, she would be a married woman right now, a prestigious lady preparing for her wedding night. She remembered how nervous Henry had been before taking her to bed. In the end, she had been the one reassuring him and taking the initiative. Somehow she guessed Philip had never suffered from similar nerves, even in preparing to bed a woman for the first time. This man was all about confidence and raw masculine power.

He would have tumbled his conquest onto the bed before she'd had time to blink and not left her side until they were both too exhausted to move.

The memory of just how skilled he was at making love to a woman sent a jolt of pleasure down her veins. It was testimony to his talent that he had managed to take her breath away when she imagined him to be a man she despised. Had she been in a more welcoming frame of mind when he had laid his hands on her, there was no telling what he might have achieved.

A cat came to stroke itself against her calf. Rose picked it up and placed it on her lap, grateful for the heat and the contented purr teasing her fingers. Edward wanted a cat. He had told her so during her last visit. And now Baron Chichester, not she, his own mother, would be the one to get it for him. The thought brought tears to her eyes.

"Oh, dear, what will I do now?" she asked the animal in a sob. "My Edward! What will he think of me?"

It broke her heart to think that as he grew up her son would think she had abandoned him, that she had allowed his grandfather to take him away from her and raise him like an orphan when he still had his mother. He would think she had not fought for him. He would never know all the sacrifices she had been prepared to make to get him back.

Perhaps it was better that he thought of her as a stranger rather than as a woman using her body to gain a husband and lying her way into marriage.

She buried her face in the animal's soft fur and cried.

The sobs twisted Philip's guts, reminding him of the

heart-wrenching cry Rose had given on the beach. Careful of remaining hidden amongst the shrubs, he walked forward and saw her hunched up, a form held tight in her arms. Once again he had unwittingly witnessed something he was not supposed to hear or see, but this time, far from angering him, the desperation in Rose's voice drew him to her. He wanted to wrap his arms around her in the same way she was hugging the cat.

What distressed her so? After the breaking off of their betrothal, he would have expected her to be angry and disappointed by the failure of her plans but not…wretched. And yet she sounded utterly crushed. Why?

It could be she was wondering what her late husband would think of her for playing such a trick on an unsuspecting man. Surely a man who had loved her would be horrified to see her plotting in such an underhanded manner, and she knew it.

Whatever the reason for it, she was distraught.

He took a step forward.

"What happened to him?" he asked softly. "Edward?" He thought she had said his name was Henry, but evidently he remembered it wrongly, for she had just called him Edward.

Rose gave a startled cry when she heard his voice. As she whipped around, the cat she was holding lifted his head. Two pairs of blue eyes, each as sharp as the other, stared at him, unblinking. The tears on Rose's cheeks—or more pointedly, the fact that she did not even try to wipe them away—made Philip uncomfortable. It was as if her distress was such that she could not even muster the energy to be ashamed.

“What did you say?” she whispered, her voice taut with tension. Evidently she did not like to talk about her late husband, but suddenly he was curious to hear about the man’s fate. How had he died?

“Edward, your husband. You were talking about him just then.” He tilted his head. “What happened to him?”

Rose shook her head, relief flooding through her. Philip did not suspect anything. He had heard her and wrongly assumed Edward to be the name of her late husband. She did not rectify his mistake and answered his question instead.

“He died at the battle of Mortimer’s Cross in February last year. I do not know much more than that. We just got his body back one day, brought back by two men who had gone to fight with him. It was…”

Fighting nausea, Rose stroked the cat’s back, remembering the horror of that moment. The animal resumed its purring under her palm, lending her some much-needed strength. Henry’s end had been unbearably brutal. The side of his head had been sliced open. Once she had seen that, she hadn’t been able to take another look at the body. For it had been just that, a body. There had been nothing left of the man she had loved, of the golden warrior she had married.

“It was awful. It was a…a corpse, it was not my husband,” she murmured. “I hardly recognized him.”

Philip could well believe it. He had seen enough men die in battle to guess what state he had been in. Still, she was lucky to have got the body back so she could give her husband a decent burial. Many of the fighters’ wives had not been granted that small mercy.

“At night I dream about how he must have felt when

he understood he was not going to survive the day," Rose carried on, wondering what was compelling her to be so honest. It felt dishonest to talk about Henry to a man who had made love to her, but she could not stop herself. Besides, after today she would never see Philip again.

"Terrified, probably. And I can't imagine the agony he must have felt when he realized that he would never see his beloved wife again, that he would never be able to say sorry for leaving you to face the aftermath of it all alone," Philip surprised her by saying. Despite the harsh picture he was painting, she felt oddly comforted to be told that Henry's last thought would have been for her.

"But that blow to his head… It is all I can think about. I hope he did not suffer." The memory of the gaping wound was so distressing that she did not think to guard her tongue and simply said what was on her mind. It was liberating to speak the words out loud, to acknowledge how the image still plagued her. "I hope he didn't have time to understand he was going to die. The worst is… He never even knew about our son, I never got the chance to tell him. He left before I found out I was with child."

It was only when Philip stared at her that Rose realized what she had just said. She had meant to keep Edward a secret, but his compassionate words had made her drop her guard.

Horrified, she stood up so swiftly the cat jumped from her lap with a shriek of protest. She made to run away, but Philip was too fast. He caught up with her before she had reached the castle walls.

He grabbed her arm and forced her to face him.

"No, Rose, wait, please. Don't go."

"Don't touch me!" she screamed. Her eyes started

to fill with tears again. She had sworn never to mention Edward to anyone, to keep her heartbreak private, and she had failed. “Please let me go,” she sobbed. To her relief Philip let go of her arm, as if he sensed that she truly could not bear to be touched by another man while she was reliving the nightmare of Henry’s death.

“You have a son,” Philip said softly, running his fingers through his hair. “And his name is Edward.”

So he had remembered correctly. *Henry* had been her husband, not Edward. For a reason that he could not fathom, the revelation affected him deeply. Imagining Rose as the mother of another man’s child so soon after being told that she was not going to give him a son was painful.

Rose wiped her tears angrily. There would be no avoiding an explanation now.

“Yes I have a son,” she said in a whisper. “He is a year old. Henry went to fight without even knowing I was with child. And now my boy will have to grow up without his father. And without his…”

And without his mother.

Pain sliced through her and would have brought her to her knees had Philip not moved to take her in his arms at that exact moment. She buried her face in his cloak and let out a wail. Oh, God, it felt so good to have someone to hold on to! It was as if having someone’s arms wrapped around her physically prevented her from falling apart. Nobody had held her thus since Henry’s death, and she could not have drawn away from Philip if her life depended on it. He infused her with his strength, allowing her to remain standing.

They remained silent for a long moment. Then her eyes snapped open. Had Philip placed a kiss on the top of her head? Before she could wonder if she had been dreaming, he spoke.

"Why will Edward have to live without you? Do you want to tell me about it?"

Rose knew she should not, but somehow the words were already on her lips. It was as if after so many months spent keeping the secret she could not contain herself a moment longer. It was ready to burst out of her.

"Henry's family never accepted our marriage, saying that I was an unsuitable wife, that he had failed his rank by marrying me. He ignored them all, and they cut his allowance to the minimum, but it didn't matter. For two years we were happy, blissfully so. But then…"

Then it had all fallen apart. At Henry's death, Baron Maltravers had stopped paying her meagre allowance, reducing her to poverty. Once his son had died, no one had been able to force him to give his despised daughter-in-law a single penny, and of course as the widow of a traitor she could not pretend to any pension.

In the end, the last, most terrible blow of all, she had lost her son.

She had not been able to stop the sequence of events, any more than she could have stopped a sandcastle from dissolving once it has been hit by a wave.

"When Edward was born, his grandfather decided he would raise him himself. I managed to hold him off for a while, though money was short, but eventually the Maltravers took him away. They know I have no resources of my own, no one to turn to for protection. They cut off my husband from the family because of his decision to be with me, but they are determined to get his heir, for all that. Had the baby been a girl, I might have been allowed to keep her," she said desolately.

"Yes, perhaps," Philip said through gritted teeth. He knew enough men of this Maltravers' ilk. The heartless bastards were only concerned about one thing—family prestige and lineage—and of course, in that game, a son was an invaluable pawn.

"They took my baby away from me. Edward was seven months old, the happiest child you could ever see. They came one morning and they just…" Rose stopped and pressed her hand to her mouth to stop the howl of pain about to come out. The memory of that moment would haunt her for the rest of her life, even if by some miracle she got Edward back one day. "I could do nothing to stop them. I have no allies."

Philip led Rose back to the bench, feeling that she needed something to support her legs. The reliving of the tragedy had taken its toll on her. He understood all too well how wretched she would feel to have her child taken from her.

There were many things he wanted to clarify, but he waited until she had regained some control over her emotions.

"By coincidence, the week after Edward was taken, your stepbrother mentioned a possible union between us," Rose carried on. "He had tried to attract my attention for a while, but I always pretended not to notice, guessing his intentions were not of the honorable kind. At any other time, I would never have even considered encouraging his advances, but my situation had changed dramatically. I could not pass up this chance to get my son back. I thought that if I was married to a man of standing, I could convince Baron Chichester that I was now able to raise Edward as befitted his rank."

Of course. It all made sense now.

"I am not sure Gilbert would have helped you," Philip murmured, a bitter taste in his mouth. "I fear you might have married him in vain."

In fact, he was sure of it. Generosity was not the man's main quality. Besides, the last thing he would have wanted was to welcome someone else's child under his roof when the situation would have reminded him of his own childhood. He would not have wanted his children to have to compete with an older stepbrother the way he'd had to deal with him.

Rose made a gesture of powerlessness. "I know that now. But I had to try. I cannot be without my son! He is so young. I have to get him back now, before it's too late. In a few months' time he will have forgotten me. The day we met on the beach, I had gone to visit him, and he barely remembered me. It had been two months since my last visit, and I do not know when I will be able to see him again!"

"That's why you were so distraught," Philip said under his breath as realization hit.

"Yes. It was not, contrary to what you assumed, because I had discovered I was with child. I swear I never meant to take advantage of you, only you appeared out of nowhere when I was racking my brain to find a solution to my problem, and I…I couldn't think. You misunderstood me, and all I could see was that once again I had been given the opportunity to ally myself with someone who would help me get Edward back." She wrung her hands together. "I'm sorry. I know I shouldn't have lied to you, but I was desperate."

"Dear God."

Philip was stunned by the enormity of the situation. He had wondered enough times why Rose had accepted

Gilbert's outrageous proposition. The notion had bothered him for months. Why had a woman like her sacrificed her dignity and allowed a man she despised access to her body? Now he knew. She had wanted to get her child back.

He remembered her utter despair at finding out that the marriage was not going to go ahead, even though she evidently did not like, much less love, Gilbert.

No wonder she had slapped him. His mistake had ruined her chance of seeing her son restored to her! In the circumstances, it was a wonder she had not run him through with a sword.

"This is why you were ready to do anything to ensure that Gilbert would marry you," he said through gritted teeth. "You were ready to sell yourself to get your son back."

She lowered her eyes in shame. "Yes."

"That's despicable."

Rose gave a gasp at Philip's choice of word but quickly understood that his contempt was aimed at his stepbrother, not at her.

"Don't feel too bad for me. In the end I never had to sell my body," she murmured. "As you know, he never laid a finger on me."

As soon as she spoke, an image of their lovemaking flashed through her mind. Sir Gilbert might not have touched her, but Philip certainly had. And she had melted. Guilt surged through her. How could she have forgotten herself in a man's arms so thoroughly, a man who was not Henry?

Perhaps it was fair that she should pay a high price for her betrayal.

"My stepbrother agreed to marry a woman who

already had a child?" Philip knew that his tone would betray his surprise, but he was dumbfounded. "I confess I would never have credited him with such generosity." Rose went red and averted her gaze, providing him with an answer. "I see," he said dryly. "It seems you were not the only one being tricked into something you did not want."

Of course Rose had not spoken about her son to Gilbert. He would never have offered her marriage otherwise, on any condition! Never would he have agreed to raise another man's child.

"I meant to tell him, I swear," Rose breathed, visibly ill at ease. "As I said, he mentioned a possible union between us just a few days after Edward had been taken away from me. I immediately accepted, and I was about to tell him about my reasons for doing so, but before I could speak out he issued his conditions as to the match." There was a pause. "Of course, after such an unsavory request, I should have made my refusal plain, and I would have in any other circumstances, but I admit that I…"

"You thought that if he was prepared to word his offer in such an insulting manner you did not owe him anything and might as well take advantage of the opportunity." Philip said out loud what she had not dared to say.

"Yes. I confess I did." Though he had spared her the humiliation of having to spell out what she had done, Rose lowered her eyes in shame. They both knew this had been underhanded behavior on her part and she deserved nothing less than his censure.

"I cannot say that I blame you," Philip said roundly, causing her to look at him in surprise. He did not seem disapproving, quite the opposite. She took in a shaky breath, relieved. “After what he’d had the gall to tell you, he didn’t deserve anything less. However, as I said, I doubt he would have lifted a finger to help you once you had finally revealed Edward’s existence.”

“Yes…” Rose had had time to realize that the two men were more like enemies than family, but it still amazed her to see that Philip would choose to side with her rather than with the man he had been raised with.

She looked at him more closely to see if she was being mistaken, but all she could see was his gleaming dark eyes. Night had fallen, and the surrounding darkness coaxed her into confiding more of her troubles. It felt good to talk about it all with someone who was lending a sympathetic ear, who was not judging her.

“I found out I was pregnant about a month after Henry’s death,” she said in a soft whisper. “I had been feeling odd for weeks, but stupidly I attributed it to the shock of knowing my husband had been killed. We had been married for less than two years when he went out to fight. We had been so happy!”

This Philip did not doubt. Living with her would be a delight. Even if Henry Maltravers had not fallen in love with Rose at first sight, it would not have taken him long to succumb to her charms. It was impossible to be near her without feeling drawn to her. He had found that out to his cost. Why, the woman had crept under his skin. They barely knew each other, he’d only come to her by mistake, she had played a nasty turn on him, and yet he was finding it impossible to stay away from her.

A man married to her, sharing her bed every night, would have found himself ensnared in no time.

“My Edward is everything I have left in this world.

The pregnancy was hard and his birth frightful. The night he was born, I thought I would lose him, and I almost died myself. I love him more than I…" She clasped her hands together and bit her trembling bottom lip.

Though he wanted to draw her into his arms, Philip again resisted the impulse. He had got away with it once, but he sensed that this time she would not allow him to treat her so intimately. They were no longer betrothed.

He had no right to her.

The notion was a knife to the gut.

"I wish Henry could have met Edward," Rose said almost to herself. "He is so much like him! I wish I could have told him he had given me a son before he left for war. Or…" Mayhap it had been for the best. Surely it would only have added to his distress to know she was with child when they parted, to know that he might never get to meet his son or daughter. "Perhaps it was for the best that he left without knowing in what situation he was leaving me," she finished.

"Yes. It would have been unbearable for him to know he was leaving when you needed him the most," Philip said in a low voice. "It is perhaps fortunate he had no inkling of the future you would face."

Rose stayed silent. Indeed. If Henry had anticipated half of what she would have to go through after his death, he would never have left. Had he imagined that his father would treat her so disdainfully, refuse her his financial help and take their son away, he would never have gone to war, even at the risk of dishonoring himself.

And if he had seen her agree to be bedded by a man who wanted to humiliate her and make another one marry her under false pretense he would have disowned her.

She gave a whimper.

Her life had become a living hell. Only in the last two days at Wicklow Castle had she been allowed a respite from the relentless worry and pain.

"In any case, it is all over now. My husband is dead, my son is gone," she told Philip, fighting back tears. What use would it be to cry? It would not change the situation.

He moved closer to her. "I would like to help."

"Please. There is nothing you can do, and no reason why you should," she breathed. "We are not betrothed any more, and I will admit that I am relieved. You did not deserve to be lied to. Taking advantage of you was eating at my insides. And…I'm sorry for the pain I caused you by pretending I was carrying your child."

He nodded slowly but said nothing. Rose lowered her head. Indeed there was nothing to say.

"I will leave Wicklow Castle in the morning. You need not worry yourself about me."

They were not to be married. He would have no reason to give her any further thought. As soon as she was gone, he would resume his life and forget this woman who had been nothing more than a mistake, in all senses of the word.

She, however, suspected she would find it hard to be free of him. If her mind would undoubtedly strive to forget him, her body would not let her. It would heat up every time she thought of him and melt when she recalled his caresses, which would only make her life even more painful than it already was.

Now she would not only miss Henry and worry about Edward, she would also hanker after someone she could not have. There was no ray of hope on the horizon.

"Please, I need a moment alone."

Philip nodded and turned away. It was hard to leave Rose alone with her grief, but he could understand she needed time to absorb everything that had happened that day. Once again she had to face the fact that she might not be reunited with her son anytime soon, if ever.

He could not think of a worse prospect for a loving mother.

Thinking hard, he made his way to the castle. They might not be getting married, but it was not over. He would find a way of helping her. *He* was not a helpless widow, by God, and he would see justice done, one way or another.

Plain Philip Whitlock had been a force to be reckoned with. Lord Chrystenden would not be denied.

Rose stared a long moment into the night, not moving, letting her body grow slowly numb. If only she could stay here until she disappeared into nothingness! She had to keep up the fight—for Edward's sake, she could not give up—but for the first time she wondered if she could do it. Never had the future appeared bleaker.

Moments later, Emeline came to coax her back inside.

"My lady, please, it is pitch dark, and getting very cold. You need to come back inside."

Did she really? Why? What difference would it make?

Dutifully she followed the girl back into the castle and to her bedchamber. Once again someone else was taking over, making decisions for her, and Rose did not have the will, much less the energy, to gainsay her. Would she ever be in control of her own destiny?

She went straight to bed, hoping sleep would bring

her some much needed oblivion.

It did not.

All night she dreamt of Henry wanting to kiss her, but the man she saw coming to her was not her beautiful husband but the frightful corpse with his gaping wound. Her screams of terror got stuck in her throat, and she woke up drenched in sweat. Oh, God, talking about Henry's death to Philip had reawakened the horror of it all. During her pregnancy she had been plagued by such vivid dreams, but thankfully it had been months since she had seen the dreadful vision.

She was so afraid of falling asleep again that she spent the rest of the night sitting at the bay window, wrapped in her blanket, shivering with despair. Unsurprisingly, she left the room at dawn with a pounding headache.

Philip watched Rose come into the great hall with shadows under her eyes and all the strength drained out of her. He had dreaded such a sight. After their discussion last night she would have spent the night mulling over the disastrous turn her life had taken.

"I will not ask if you slept well," he said quietly.

She managed a taut smile, one that tugged at his heart. "No."

"You need to eat something," he told her, taking her arm. "Come."

He'd asked for a veritable feast to be prepared, in the hope of tempting her appetite, but she hardly touched a thing. The contrast with the previous mornings when she had devoured everything with a smile on her face was painful. Even if he had not already decided to help her, he would have done so there and then. Rose could not waste away while she worried about her son. As her husband, it would have been his duty to look after her wellbeing, and he intended to do just that, regardless of whether they were married or not.

No one else would come forward.

"I will not be taking Emerald with me," Rose said quietly, placing her eating knife back on the table. This gift had been intended for the future Lady Chrystenden, and she would never be that woman. She had no right to it. "I thank you for the present, but you must see why I cannot keep her."

Philip gave her a long stare, and she had the impression he was about to protest. Then, to her relief, he relented. "If you insist."

"I do."

"A litter will be made ready for you when you are ready. Please take as much time as you need. I have some urgent business to attend to, so I will be leaving shortly, but there is no need for you to leave in a hurry."

Once he was gone, Rose's feet took her to the stables, and Emerald.

"I'm sorry I cannot take you with me," she told the mare, placing her forehead against the warm neck. Yet another parting, yet another thing she was losing… When would it end? The animal neighed softly, as if it understood everything she was not saying.

After one last stroke on the soft nose, Rose made her way to the litter.

Lord Chrystenden was behaving with more thoughtfulness than his stepbrother, she noted, which came as no surprise. Once Sir Gilbert had broken their betrothal, he had sent her away unceremoniously, in shame, not giving her safety any thought. Philip, by contrast, had taken care to provide her with every comfort. Nonetheless, he was sending her away with no hope of reconciliation.

He had not even come to bid her farewell. The message was clear. He was done with her.

Rose's throat felt too tight to swallow properly. She stared fixedly ahead of her when the litter jolted forward, refusing to take a last look at Wicklow Castle, the place she would never call her own. So this was it. She would never see Philip again.

What could possibly have kept him away from saying good bye to a woman he had almost married? He had alluded to urgent business requiring his attention when he had eaten with her, before leaving the great hall already booted and spurred like a man who would not suffer a moment's delay. She could not fathom what that urgent matter might be, for if everything had gone according to plan, this would have been the morning after their wedding night. Would he have left his newly married wife at the first chance?

Mayhap. In view of his sudden departure, she was forced to conclude that he had never intended to stay with her once the ceremony was completed. It could be that he considered their marriage already consummated, of course, which it was. And if he was convinced she was already with child, there would have been no incentive to bed her in order to get an heir. It might also be that he feared hurting the babe if he took her to bed.

Evidently this marriage would never have been anything other than a marriage of convenience to him. He was doing his duty by her because he was an honorable man, but he had no intention of being a true husband to her. He would marry to repair the wrong he had unwittingly caused her, but he would do no more; he would not change his life to accommodate his new wife.

Regrets filled Rose. She could live with foregoing the advantages being Lady Chrystenden would have given her, as a prestigious status had never been what she hankered after, but renouncing a marriage based on mutual respect and understanding was a much more bitter pill to swallow. The way Philip had taken her in his arms the day before had warmed a part of her soul no one had touched since Henry's death.

The knowledge that she would never be anyone's cherished wife ever again chilled her to the core.

Her hand found its way to her stomach. Her pregnancy with Edward had been difficult, his birth excruciatingly painful, but she longed for other children to love. Other children that would never be taken away from her, that would be allowed to grow by her side.

It would not happen now. The night she had spent in Philip's arms had happened three months ago, long enough for her to know for certain she was never going to give him a child.

Everything was indeed falling apart.

Henry was dead, she was not pregnant, she was not going to marry Philip, and Edward would never be restored to her.

She was alone. Forever alone.

Chapter 8

"Lord Chrystenden!"

Rose watched in amazement as Philip jumped down from his horse and walked toward her. Though seeing him was the last thing she had expected, she could not have mistaken him. No two men possessed such commanding presence. His features were set in a stern expression, but she quickly saw that anger was not the cause of it, rather something akin to deadly intent. He looked like a man on a mission, even if she could not imagine what that mission might be.

"I see that you will persist in not calling me Philip," he said once he had come to a halt in front of her.

Of course she would not call him Philip! He had once told her that he would like them to use their Christian names, but this had been when they were betrothed. She had no reason to be so familiar with him now.

"What are you doing here?" she asked, not knowing how to behave or what to think.

To say that this visit was unexpected would be an understatement. She had spent the best part of the morning at the village, helping the women to make cheese, and now felt at a disadvantage. Had she known he would come today, she would have changed into a more presentable gown. But how could she have suspected he would ever visit her? It had been two weeks since their last encounter, and she had spent every moment of every day trying to persuade herself that she would never see him again, and that it suited her fine.

Now he was here, all masculine beauty and forbidding intent, she had to acknowledge that she had been fooling herself.

"I came to give you this."

With those words he handed her a piece of paper. With its big waxed seal, it looked official, as official and impressive as Philip himself. His tunic of dark velvet made him appear darker himself, and he was wearing a hat adorned with a brooch. She had never seen him in such magnificent apparel. He was dressed in a manner more suited to a visit to court than to an impoverished widow in the country.

"What is it?" she asked, looking at the paper. She could not quite bring herself to touch it.

"It is an ordinance from King Edward." There was a pause. "Your pension has been restored to you. You do not need to wait for charity from Baron Maltravers or anyone else. From this day hence, you will be, if not exactly a rich woman, at least comfortable enough to get your son back."

Rose's mouth opened in shock. Get her son back? She had hoped to hear these exact words so many times, but now that she had…they didn't seem real.

"Why… The king…" She was speechless. "Why would he do this for me? I never petitioned him. I do not know him."

"No, but I do. I asked for an audience with him. That is why I left so abruptly the morning you left Wicklow Castle, something I did not even apologize for," Philip said. He gritted his teeth. How had he not thought she would be hurt by his apparent desertion? He'd had a good reason for leaving her at such an inopportune moment, but of course Rose had not known that. She would have thought him as callous as Gilbert, sending her away without so much as a good bye.

"By chance I had heard the day before that he was on progress in a nearby town," he explained. "The opportunity was too good to miss, and I had to leave without delay. I did not tell you at the time because I did not want to raise your hopes too much in case I could not gain access to him. But I did, and here is the result."

"You went to the king to petition on my behalf and ask for my pension to be restored?" Rose wasn't sure she'd heard him correctly. But Philip nodded as if this was the most natural thing in the world.

"I fought for him in various battles and was made a lord for my services. He was kind enough to remember me and grant me this small favor. Our sovereign is a generous and forgiving man. I argued that a widow could not be made accountable for her husband's unfortunate allegiances and promised that you would not use your influence to foment rebellion against him. I trust you not to make a fool out of me now and raise an army to bring him down."

His lips quivered. They both knew that she had no influence and would never pose any threat to the king, but he enjoyed teasing her. She had a ready sense of humor and was not easily prone to offense. It was one of the things that had drawn him to her and what he had missed the most.

Rose understood Philip was teasing her, as was his wont, but she could not smile back. She was too dumbstruck, too touched that he would have taken the trouble to risk angering the king, all for her.

"Why would you do this for me?"

The brown eyes glittered. "Apart from an innate sense of justice, you mean? What happened to you is appalling. I do not see that an innocent woman should be punished and pay all her life for her husband's decisions in such an extreme fashion, when we all know that more often than not she has no input in them and may not agree with them."

"Yes, apart from that," Rose whispered. Though she could readily believe that Philip would be moved by such a situation, she had a feeling that he had meant to help because of who she was, not for a mere question of principle.

His next words confirmed it.

"I think you will agree that I owed it to you. I was the one who, albeit unwittingly, denied you the solution you had found to your predicament. I still do not agree that you should have married Gilbert, so I cannot be too sorry about being the cause of his change of heart, but I can feel responsible for the consequences." He pursed his lips like a man who had eaten an unripe fruit by accident and could not get the tart taste out of his mouth. "I could not in all conscience have left it at that, after hearing your story. This is for little Edward as much as for you."

The declaration brought a lump to Rose's throat. By rights, Philip should not have wanted to have anything to do with her after the trick she had played on him. She had lied to him, pretended to carry his child, allowed him to pamper her like a proud father-to-be, and taken advantage of his generosity.

And then she had crushed his hopes.

The pain in his eyes when he'd realized she was not pregnant after all was impossible to forget. It was something she would feel guilty about for the rest of her life.

"Forgive me, but I thought you would be pleased," Philip said when she remained silent. "You can go to Henry's father and claim your son back, now that you have the means to raise him. The proof of it is in your hand, signed by the king himself. You could go today, if you wanted to."

The lump in Rose's throat grew even bigger. Philip was trying to help, but he had not understood the situation.

"I may have the financial means to take care of Edward, but I still do not have the right lineage or connections," she said, forcing the humiliating words out. The last thing she wanted was for Philip to think she was ungrateful, but she had to face reality. "A boy raised by me will never have the prestigious upbringing Baron Chichester wants for his heir. He will contest this."

She looked at the piece of paper in her hand and felt more wretched than she had ever felt. This should be more than enough to get Edward back, but she knew it would not suffice. Her shoulders slumped. Philip had gone to all this trouble for nothing.

"He will not dare say anything if I come with you and tell him that it is the king's express wish that your son be returned to his mother," he answered with superb arrogance.

"Did the king tell you this?" Rose asked in bewilderment. "He personally asked you to help me get my son back?" Generous as he was reported to be, she could not imagine the monarch of all England bothering himself with someone as insignificant as she was.

"No, he did not. But I do not remember him forbidding it, either," Philip admitted with one of his most mischievous smiles. "Baron Chichester doesn't stand a chance. I am not a man to be thwarted, and the mighty Lord Chrystenden doesn't have any time to waste in petty confrontations."

The way he said his name made her smile. He was enjoying himself, and for the first time Rose allowed herself to hope. If he truly was prepared to help her, then her father-in-law would have no choice but to relent. With "the mighty Lord Chrystenden" on her side, Henry's family would not dare go against her wishes. The man was impressive enough, and he had the ear of the king—he had procured the ordinance for her.

She bit her lip. Could she ask him for yet another favor, after what he had done for her?

"Yes…if you came with me, then I think it might work," she said, breathless with hope.

"It will. Rest assured that I will not have a moment's peace until I have seen you reunited with your son." All amusement was gone. His words sounded like an oath.

Rose looked around her. "Would you be ready to leave immediately?"

"If such is your wish." A little bow accompanied the words.

"It is. Let us set off now."

Her heart nearly burst at the idea of holding Edward in her arms before the day was out. She hadn't seen him in more than four weeks. Her father-in-law had ignored her numerous letters requesting a visit. On the single occasion she had taken a chance and gone without invitation, she had been told they were visiting Baron

Chichester's cousin in London.

She refused to think they would not be at home today.

"It is still early. If there are no difficulties, we could be back here before nightfall…"

Philip did not even hesitate. "There won't be any difficulties, trust me."

His very confidence reassured her. Tonight Edward would sleep under her roof, in the room she had prepared for him. The thought made her dizzy with joy, and she had to stop herself from running to the stables there and then.

"Let us go." Philip offered her his arm.

"But, it's…" Rose came to an abrupt halt. A golden horse was tethered to the hoop on the wall of the stables, a horse that did not belong to her.

"Yes. I am returning Emerald to you," Philip said tranquilly, as if there was nothing extraordinary in the fact. "She is of no use to me, as no one has managed to ride her since you left. I told you of her temper. I was not wrong. It seems you are the only one she will accept on her back."

This was an exaggeration, and even if the horse was difficult he could easily have sold her on, but he had been unable to part from her. He had known from the start that he would return her to Rose one day, if simply for the pleasure of seeing her atop the gleaming animal.

The two of them belonged together.

"Please do not refuse. It was inconvenient enough to lead her behind me once. I do not wish for a repeat of the performance on my way back to Wicklow Castle," he added with a grimace.

She smiled, and he saw that she would not refuse his

gift. She was too enamored with the mare and too eager to set off without any unnecessary delays. Philip noted how she had not taken the time to get changed out of her rumpled clothes, such was her haste to be reunited with her son.

"I am very touched, and very grateful to you for making it look as if you had no choice but to return her to me," she said, proving she had seen to the heart of his lie.

"I told you. I am not a man to be thwarted in my wishes. The horse is yours, whether you ride it or not. Now let us set off."

He watched her climb atop the mare, with undisguised admiration. Her complexion was rosy, her eyes sparkled like precious gems, and her mien was more assured than it had ever been. He had never seen her look more alive or more desirable. She was a new woman, radiant with happiness. If he'd had any doubt whether he was doing the right thing, one look at her transformation would have been enough to convince him.

By ensuring he could return her son to her, he had changed her life.

Sitting on top of Emerald, she presented as striking a picture as he had hoped. The mare let out a whinny of satisfaction, as if order had been restored. It was a feeling he understood all too well—it was the same for him. He could have watched them for days on end but, understandably, Rose was itching to go. He would have to leave the admiring to another time.

"Lead the way, my lady," he said, kicking his horse into a trot.

****

The journey passed in a blur, with an impatient Rose

urging Emerald on over fences and ditches as if they were no more than rabbit holes.

Philip had rarely enjoyed himself more. Rose was a competent rider, and happiness made her reckless. The mare was only too glad to be given free rein, and by the time they came back down to a trot she was panting hard.

They drew up at the gate of a castle of impressive proportions just as the sun finally managed to burst through the clouds. Not a man prone to see meaning in such events, Philip fought hard to suppress the urge to see this as a sign that their endeavor was looked upon favorably. He was definitely doing the right thing by reuniting Rose and Edward.

"Here we are."

A shapely leg was revealed when Rose jumped down from her horse in a manner betraying her haste more than her breeding. Philip hid a smile and promised himself the pleasure of standing by the mare when she climbed back onto the saddle. Her heart would be so filled with joy that she would surely afford him another glimpse of her calf.

Though they had slept together, it had been pitch dark in the room. He now realized that he had not had the delight of seeing any part of her body except the ones available to anyone, and he was desperate to see more than her hands and face, graceful though they might be.

But how? How would he ever be given the opportunity to take her to bed? He would not be able to claim ignorance of who she was a second time, and they were not betrothed any more. She was out of his reach, as surely as if she had gone to live abroad.

Pushing these unhelpful thoughts away from his mind, he handed his horse to the waiting groom and followed Rose across a well-maintained courtyard. The contrast with her dilapidated manor was glaring. This was an opulent family's seat of power.

Still, little Edward would never be happier here than he would be with a mother like Rose.

A man came out of the great hall as they were about to enter it. The icy stare he gave Rose told Philip he must be none other than Baron Chichester, her once father-in-law. After what he had heard about him, he had not imagined he would find him amenable, but he had not expected to feel such an instant dislike toward him. The man managed to appear both full of contempt and dangerous, an explosive combination. He braced himself for the inevitable confrontation, determined to be the one on the receiving end of the baron's violence if need be.

"What do you want?"

No word of greeting. The atmosphere was as tense as Rose had described. From the stiffening of her stance he could tell she was expecting an argument. He could only agree with her. The man's glare spelt trouble.

He placed himself slightly to the side to allow her to deal with the situation as she deemed fit, but he remained alert. At the least provocation he would pounce. If the man dared to touch her, it would be the last thing he ever did.

"I am here to take Edward back," Rose announced without preamble, intent on putting the whole episode behind her as swiftly as possible.

"Take my grandson? Have you taken leave of your senses?" Baron Chichester eyed her up and down with a grimace. Evidently he had seen her sullied gown and thought she looked more like a dairymaid than a woman who had once been married to his son. She bit her lip in dismay, wishing she had taken the time to change. She had not realized just how unsuitable her appearance was because Philip had not passed any comment on it.

All she had seen in his eyes was admiration.

The thought lent her strength. If he didn't object to her appearance, why should she worry about what her father-in-law thought of her? After today they would never see each other again.

"I have never been better, thank you, since I will be taking my son back home with me," she repeated firmly.

"Not if I have any say in it."

"You do not. These are the king's orders."

The man gave a snort. "The king's orders, no less! Do you expect me to believe that?"

"No." Rose gave a tight little smile. She had fully anticipated his reluctance, and yet she was still irritated by it. "This, however, will not be ignored."

She handed him the sealed order, realizing only then that she had not even read it, trusting Philip's word implicitly. Of course her father-in-law did no such thing. He broke the seal and read the parchment attentively. A smile appeared on his lips as he did.

"This is of no concern to me. It doesn't say anything about you getting my grandson. It merely reinstates your rights as a widow."

"Which means I will now have the means to raise Edward," she argued.

"No. All that means is that you will finally be able to buy yourself suitable clothes instead of wandering around in peasant garments." His gaze wandered up and down her body contemptuously, and Rose did her best not to squirm. "But there is nothing in here that can force me to hand my grandson over to you," he said with finality.

Rose's face fell. Indeed there wasn't. She had no means of pressure over Baron Chichester. Even with money she was just as powerless as she had ever been. The idea that she might not after all get to leave with her son was enough to make her waver on her feet. Behind her she felt Philip come forward, a comforting presence.

"There is nothing in that document referring to the lady's son, but I am here to ensure that the king's command is carried out. If she now deems it possible for her to raise him as befitting his rank, then her decision is paramount and will have to be respected."

"Will it, by God! And who might you be?"

Philip bowed as if he had not noticed the blatant rudeness.

"Philip Whitlock, Lord Chrystenden, at your service," he answered with all the grace of a courtier. "His Majesty has seen it fit to grant the Lady Rose her widow's pension and intends that her son be restored to her without further ado if such is her wish."

"It is," Rose confirmed, taking a step forward.

The man ignored her completely. "The king would entrust the future Baron Chichester to this woman's care, when her husband was a known traitor to his cause? Is he not afraid that she will raise him as a rebel?"

Philip's blood boiled in his veins. Baron Chichester would be brought to heel for calling Rose, the mother of his grandson, "this woman" with such cold contempt, if for nothing else. Henry had been his son, yet he'd referred to him as "her husband" as if he had washed his hands of him. Such a heartless bastard would not be allowed to raise Edward.

He had heard enough and was eager to be gone.

"King Edward hopes that Lady Rose will have seen the error of her husband's way and that, grateful to her rightful sovereign for his merciful pardon, she will raise her son in the love and respect his subjects owe His Majesty. It is of utmost importance therefore that little Edward be handed over to her without delay. We all know that a boy's allegiances are decided in his infancy."

Baron Chichester blanched. Indeed the attack was blunt. Philip was hinting that if Henry had fought on the wrong side at Mortimer's Cross, the fault for it lay with his own father. He was also suggesting that Edward would in turn be raised a traitor if he remained in his grandfather's custody, something the king could not allow.

The man was a bully, but he was not an idiot. He knew he did not have any choice but to give in. Harboring Lancastrian sympathies was a dangerous thing to do in this climate, and he would have to surrender if he did not want aspersions made about his loyalty to the crown.

Rose watched the events unfold with intense satisfaction. How many times had she longed to see her father-in-law brought to heel!

The hope she had placed in Philip was fully justified. He had sprung up in her defense unprompted and all but accused Baron Chichester of treason! She barely repressed a smile. With just a few chosen words, he had won. The fight was over before it had even begun.

Her heart leapt in happiness and gratitude.

"In any case, I do not see why we are having this discussion. I think you will agree that the king does not have to justify his decisions to you or indeed anyone. If he wishes for the lady's son to be restored to her, then it shall be so, whatever his motives," Philip said to put an end to the matter. His tone brooked no protest. "Kindly ask for Master Edward to be brought forthwith. We do not wish to be on the road after sundown. It will not do to expose a child to unnecessary dangers. As his grandfather, you must agree."

There was no gainsaying Lord Chrystenden in this inflexible mood. Rose could only marvel at this demonstration of absolute self-confidence. She had never seen her father-in-law so discomfited before, and she enjoyed the experience immensely.

Then she forgot everything, for she saw her son running toward her, and her heart exploded in her chest. She fell to her knees and hugged him against her.

"Edward, my boy. My love," she murmured into his soft hair, kissing him on the forehead, on the cheeks, on the nose, everywhere. He smelt so good and felt so warm in her arms! Rose knew she would always remember this moment of pure, unaltered joy. She was finally reunited with her son! They would never be parted now.

"Mama."

Oh, it wasn't too late! He hadn't forgotten her! She buried her face in the crook of his neck and screwed her eyes shut, fighting tears, feeling happier than she had ever been.

Philip watched the little boy with his arms wound tight around his mother's neck and had an image of what he must have looked like himself as a child. He had not been much older than Edward when his own mother had died, and he had no memory of her. But he imagined she would have held him in her arms with just as much love.

Baron Chichester gave an impatient cough, but Rose didn't react. She had forgotten everything that wasn't her son. With a smile, Philip placed a hand on her shoulder to bring her back to the present.

Rose started when she felt a warm hand land on her shoulder. Slightly dazed, she lifted her head to Philip.

"My lady, it is time to go." His eyes were warm with approval, not impatience. Of course. What was she doing? There would be time for embraces later. For now, they had to leave this wretched place.

She rose up and addressed herself to her son.

"Edward, you are coming back with me today. We must leave immediately if we are to arrive home before nightfall." She placed a hand on his head. "Let us thank Baron Chichester for his care of you and be on our way without further ado."

Graciousness cost her little now that she was assured of getting her son back. Then the hand on Edward's hair froze and she looked around her in dismay. In her haste, she had not given the matter of the little boy's transport any thought. Aged just over a year old, he could not ride, and she had not brought anything that might serve to carry him back to home.

Baron Chichester saw the expression on her face and smiled. "Perhaps the boy should remain here until you have organized adequate transport for him. For his safety, you understand," he added in a syrupy voice. "As his grandfather, I agree that it will not do to expose a child to unnecessary dangers."

Rose's heart plummeted in her chest. After having imagined that her son would sleep in his own bed tonight, it was a hard setback. She could not bear the idea of Edward staying a moment longer under his grandfather's roof. But she refused to be defeated so easily. If he was to stay here tonight, then at least she would stay with him.

She was about to tell him as much when Philip spoke.

"Adequate transport has already been arranged. Master Edward is to ride with me," he interposed with more than a hint of irritation. "Why else do you think I came all this way? To ensure that you would do your duty by your king? It never entered anyone's mind that you would not do so. You had better make sure I do not report anything different."

"No. Of course not."

"Good. Now, let us go before you start questioning my ability to ride safely with a child in front of me. Needless to say, I would not take it too kindly."

There was no more to be said. This time Baron Chichester was well and truly beaten. Rose threw Philip a grateful glance. Once again he had smoothed the path for her.

"Good bye, Edward."

There were no embraces, no terms of endearment or even words of advice. After this cold dismissal, Baron Chichester turned and disappeared into the great hall. Edward did not call after him.

"What did I tell you? No trouble." Philip winked at Rose. The gesture was so intimate, so tender, that she felt her insides become liquid. No, no trouble, indeed. Did the man ever experience failure? "The baron should not bother you again," he added when she remained silent.

"No." Her heart lifted at the thought.

"Now, do you trust me to ride with your son?"

"Of course." She would have trusted him with her life.

Philip vaulted into the saddle. Without the least

hesitation, she handed Edward to him. She had never ridden with a small child in her arms and was not quite sure how to manage. Her son would be safer with Philip than he was even with her, his own mother.

"Oh, Mama! Big horse!"

From his vantage point, Edward looked overawed, and Rose could not help a laugh at the delight on his face.

Philip smiled. The weight of the warm little body pressed against his chest was so comforting that he barely resisted the impulse to kiss the top of the boy's hair. His heart leapt in remembrance. How many times had he ridden thus with little Emma settled against him?

He could still hear her tinkling laugh in his ear. His chest constricted in emotion, and he tightened his fingers on the reins.

"Let us go, Master Edward. You give the word when you are ready."

Chapter 9

"I don't know how to thank you for what you did today," Rose said, sitting herself next to Philip.

He raised a hand in a gesture she would have recognized anywhere. No one was more modest in victory than he was. Yet what he had done could never be repaid. She had just tucked a sleepy Edward into bed and spent a long moment by his side, just watching his chest rise and fall.

"Please. I assure you the pleasure of seeing you and your son together was ample reward for my efforts. And now at last my conscience is clear. You will not have to marry anyone you do not want just so you can get Edward back." His dark eyes glittered.

With a pang of dismay Rose understood that he was placing himself in the same category as his stepbrother, a man she had resigned herself to marry when her whole self rebelled at the idea. But she did not see the two men in the same way at all.

If she was relieved beyond measure to be reunited with her son without having become Sir Gilbert's wife, her feelings about her doomed union to Philip were of a very different nature. She had spent weeks doing her best to convince herself that she would forget him—without ever managing to do so. In fact, her craving for him had increased with each passing day.

The thought that she would have liked to be his wife

even if she'd had nothing to gain from it had crossed her mind on more than one occasion. She would have been happy to be married to Philip for all sorts of reasons, and not all of them had to do with the comfort and protection he would provide her. He truly was a man like no other. He aroused, amused, and intrigued her all at once.

But one thing was bothering her. She decided to get to the bottom of it without further ado.

"Why were you so set on helping me get Edward back?" she asked bluntly. A direct man himself, Philip would appreciate her forthrightness. "I can see it is not only so that your conscience would be clear. You are like a man on a mission."

"I confess that I didn't think you would question my motives for helping you, as long as I did," Philip said in an unusually deep voice. "How very clever of you to have noticed I had my own reasons for doing so."

With any other man, this comment might have sounded condescending, but the light in his eyes was too bright for her to be fooled. He was not mocking her but teasing her, as usual, and enjoying it.

"Yes, well, I am rather perceptive when I want to be. For example, I cannot help but notice that you haven't answered my question." She smiled, but she could tell the explanation to his unusual doggedness would be something very personal and that was why he was stalling. Still she was desperate to know.

It was true Philip had not expected Rose to bother herself with his motives, but he was glad she had asked. It showed she saw him as more than a tool to be used for her advantage. Now that Edward was returned to her, she could have considered that what he thought did not matter as long as she had benefited from it. He took the time to consider his response carefully before he answered her. They had retired to a corner of the great hall, and the light from the dwindling fire did not quite reach them. Darkness was surrounding them, and everything was quiet. At that precise moment they seemed to be the only two people in the world.

He stretched his legs in front of him.

"There are various reasons for me helping you. I told you one of them. I do not think it fair that a woman should pay all her life for a choice her husband made, nor do I believe that a child should ever be separated from his mother when neither deserve such a fate."

Philip paused. Rose kept her eyes on him, making the most of the fact that he was staring into the distance. He was…beautiful. The word was perhaps odd for a man as dark and virile as he was, but it was all she could think.

"Since I was made a lord, I have had ample opportunity to see that such distinction is a largely empty honor," he said, taking her by surprise.

"Empty!" she could not help but exclaim. She knew many men who would have given their right arm for such a title.

"Yes, empty," Philip asserted, looking at her squarely. "I have never hankered after social recognition. This is not how I measure a man's worth. I did not fight for the king expecting rewards. I fought because I believed his cause to be right. But finally, today, it meant something to have the ear of the king. I was able to do something that actually matters. I care not for being called 'my lord' instead of 'Philip' by people who do not know me, but I do care about having power if it enables me to right something I see as wrong."

Rose waited. There was more to come, she was sure

of it. A log fell in the hearth, sending sparks everywhere. Philip stood up and went to stir the embers. Then he placed both his hands flat on the wall in front of him and leaned against it. The muscles on his shoulders rippled as he did so.

Rose swallowed hard. Yes, he was so beautiful, and…so strong.

"I cannot help but see myself in Edward," he said suddenly, turning to face her.

"Do you?" This was the last thing she had expected him to say. "But…he looks nothing like you!"

Philip planted his gaze into hers, and she flushed. They were both thinking that he had once thought she would bear a child that would look just like him.

He gave a slanted smile. "No, I know he doesn't. You told me he takes after his father. I take it, then, that Henry was blond with blue eyes, the opposite of me. But that is not what I mean. You know Gilbert is only my stepbrother. We have the same mother but not the same father. When I was only a few months old, my real father died."

The flat voice told Rose that he had no feelings for that man he had never known. It pierced her heart to think that one day Edward would feel the same about Henry, but she forced this unhelpful consideration out of her mind to listen to him.

"At his death, my mother found herself with a small son to raise and no means of support. Mayhap her situation will stir some compassion within you," Philip said wryly. "You seem to have a lot in common with her."

Though she could tell Philip had not meant to sound accusatory, Rose lowered her eyes in shame.

"Did she manipulate your stepfather into marrying her and impose her son onto him as I would have?" she murmured. "Did she use her body to buy his protection?"

"No, she did not," he answered in a deep rumble.

"Then we do not have much in common. Your mother had more dignity and honor than I've ever had. Don't pretend you don't remember what I did."

Philip walked over to her, then slowly dropped to one knee so their eyes were level. Intent etched on his face, he cupped her cheek with his hand.

"Rose, listen to me. My mother did not manipulate anyone or sell herself to an unscrupulous man because, unlike you, she didn't need to," he said softly. "My stepfather was in love with her, and mercifully I hadn't been taken away from her. If I had, I am sure she would have done exactly the same as you, and more. A mother will do whatever it takes to ensure her child's future happiness, and thank God for it, for who else would do it?"

A candle was lit, but it was placed behind Philip. Only the flickering flames in the hearth shed any light on his face, making his eyes glow like embers. Rose gulped. The moment was deeply intimate, and uncomfortably so. For a long moment Philip just stared at her without speaking. He was at her feet, and her face was still cradled in his palm. When his thumb drew circles on her cheekbone, her whole body started to dissolve.

She stood up, unable to deal with it all, and poured herself a cup of small ale with shaking hands. The liquid hitting her throat restored some sense into her.

"So it is a happy family story after all." She had had her doubts on the matter. Philip's opinion of his stepbrother did not seem to indicate a happy childhood.

"No. Not quite. My mother died shortly after giving birth to Gilbert, you see. I have no memory of her," he said, standing up in turn.

Something constricted inside Rose's chest. He had no memories of either of his parents… What a sad story.

"So you were left alone with a man who wasn't your father and a stepbrother who hates you. How you must have suffered…" She handed him a cup of ale. He took it and gave a slanted smile.

"Once again, not quite. My stepfather, Sir Thomas, was a model of generosity and honor. He raised me as his own son. As I said, he had loved my mother deeply, and he wanted to ensure that her boy would come to no harm. I cannot praise him enough for it, but I do not think that the love he had borne her accounted solely for his decision. You see, he was a fundamentally fair and selfless man and would have done his duty by me whatever the circumstances. I am proud to have been his son."

Rose contemplated this for a moment. Philip's stepfather had been a fair, selfless, and honorable man. Now she knew from whence he had gotten these traits.

"I can only imagine the poor man's disillusion upon seeing that his true son had not inherited any of his qualities, while his stepson was the very embodiment of the man he would have wanted to raise," she mused.

Philip twisted his mouth. "You *are* perceptive, my lady."

She smiled back. "So I'm right."

"You are, and this, of course, only contributed to the feeling of enmity between Gilbert and me. He always resented the way our father seemed to prefer my company." Rose noticed the way he called Gilbert's father his own so naturally. "It made him predisposed to be wary of me, and I confess that in turn I never forgave him for not living up to our father's expectations. We never got on. At first I tried to create a bond with him, this brother who was only two years younger than me, but it never worked. Eventually I stopped trying to be in his good graces."

"I suppose Sir Gilbert never tried to establish any relationship with you." It was not difficult to imagine that Philip would have been the one making all the effort.

"No. Of course the fact that we are as different as could be did not help."

Rose could only nod. One dark, one fair, one taut and energetic, one plump and indolent—never had two men looked more dissimilar. And the physical difference between them was just the outside manifestation of their contrasting personalities. She could not think of a single thing they had in common. Sir Gilbert was as selfish and mean as Philip was generous and kind.

"When our father died, I was fourteen and Gilbert twelve. He became the new master of Harleith Castle and, young as he was, he made my life hell. At least he tried to, for I was not such a willing victim. But his status as a legitimate son afforded him many privileges, and not many stood up to defend me." There Philip made a grimace, betraying the pain that people's defection had caused him. "Not everyone is as open-minded as my stepfather, and many thought he had been far too generous toward a boy who was not of his getting."

"Of course," Rose murmured. She knew all there was to know about people's meanness toward those they did not deem worthy of their esteem.

"In just a few years, Gilbert made my situation there

untenable. I left Harleith Castle as soon as I was able. I joined the forces of King Edward, who was then the Earl of March and only a pretender to the throne. He rewarded me with the title of Lord in July when he was crowned. I gambled my future, trusting this charismatic young man, trusting he would prove a victorious fighter and a grateful monarch. Fortunately, I was right."

"Sir Gilbert must have been rather put out to see you elevated so!" The thought pleased her.

"Yes. Very." Philip smiled as though the idea afforded him the same pleasure, and she thought she had never seen a man in possession of such a sunny smile. It was irresistible. "I confess that witnessing his outrage pleased me immensely, almost more than the title itself."

"He never mentioned your new title when we discussed a possible union between us," Rose observed. "In fact he only ever mentioned you once in passing."

"That does not surprise me. My very existence is the bane of Gilbert's life. If only I could have died in battle, he would have been…" Philip stopped when he saw Rose bite the inside of her mouth and cursed himself for this indelicate comment. Of course she would be thinking of her husband, who had actually died on the battlefield. "I'm sorry, I should not have said that."

"It's all right. And I know what you meant." Undoubtedly, Sir Gilbert would have preferred for his hated, more accomplished brother never to come back from war.

Rose shook her head and decided to change the subject before the atmosphere became too awkward. Tonight Philip and she were sharing a moment of unexpected intimacy, making her realize that she did not know anything about the man she had almost married—

and already bedded.

It was a risky game to play because the more she found out about him the more fascinated she grew, and she was already in danger of falling for him. He lifted his chin, and that simple move was so seductive that she cleared her throat.

Yes, she should definitely retire to her bedchamber before things got out of hand…

She stayed where she was and poured herself another cup of ale.

"What was it you overheard that day?" she asked, suddenly remembering what he had told her the day he had broken their engagement. When he had first mentioned it, it had not been the right moment to ask questions about it, but she had wondered about it ever since. "It has something to do with your stepbrother, hasn't it?"

Philip smiled, as if he had guessed it would not be long before she gave in to curiosity.

"Yes, of course it does. Everything that happened to me during my childhood has something to do with Gilbert, in one way or another." He gave a snort. "I was twelve. I had gone to see my horse in the stables, as he had been injured earlier that day and I wanted to see how he was doing. As I was bending over to check its leg, Gilbert walked in with his friend Lord Woton's son. Because of my position behind the horse, they did not see me. It soon became clear that I had better stay hidden and listen to their conversation. They were discussing a trick they wanted to play on me."

Rose nodded. She had guessed it would be something like that. Sir Gilbert was nothing if not underhanded. "And the dog?"

"You remember that detail?" Philip sounded amused, but she remembered everything he had ever told her. "Yes. There is a dog involved in the story. The two of them were planning on injuring our father's favorite greyhound and leaving him to bleed to death. Gilbert has always had a streak of cruelty in him," he added when she gasped at the appalling revelation. "Forgive me, I did not think that this would come as a surprise to you."

"No." She had seen enough of him to believe Philip unconditionally, even though what he said was a horrifying plan, coming from a ten-year old boy.

"That hound had bitten me earlier that week during a hunt. Gilbert explained to his friend that if he could convince our father that I had injured the dog in retaliation, it would mark a turning point in our relationship. After such a stunt, I was sure to lose his respect and affection." Philip remained calm, but she could see the hurt, the anger, boiling under the surface. His hand automatically went to the hilt of his sword, something he often did when he talked about his stepbrother.

"Would it have worked?" Surely a man who loved Philip so well and trusted him would never have believed him capable of such a horrific deed.

Philip shrugged. He had often wondered the same thing himself. Would Sir Thomas have believed him in preference to his own son? He liked to think his father would have trusted his word when he denied any wrongdoing, but he could not be sure.

"I certainly hope not, but I cannot say. In any case, I found the dog before they could, then went to my father and explained everything. We both went to confront the boys. Under questioning, Gilbert kept his cool, but Lord

Woton's son crumbled and admitted everything."

He clenched his jaw. It had been difficult to witness the crushing disappointment in his father's eyes as he had understood what sort of spiteful individual his natural son truly was. Had there been any other way of proving his innocence, Philip would have taken it, as he knew exposing Gilbert's treacherous nature could only pain the man, but he had not been able to find one.

From that day onward, something had changed between Gilbert and his father, something that had inevitably made the two brothers' relationship even more strained. Nevertheless, on his deathbed Sir Thomas had made Philip promise he would never give up on his stepbrother. To the last, he had hoped his son would one day come to see the error of his ways and grow up to be a worthy individual.

Though he knew this would never happen, Philip had promised not to cut all relations with Gilbert. It was the least he could do to ease the conscience of a man who had given him such a chance in life. Without this binding promise, he would have washed his hands of Gilbert the moment his father was buried. As it was, he went back to Harleith Castle regularly, something that never failed to inflame the situation between the two men even further.

It would be worse from now on. After the way he had treated Rose, Philip would never be able to give Gilbert the benefit of the doubt ever again.

It was fortunate their father had died before he'd heard the sorry tale of his son pressuring a desperate lady into sleeping with him before their marriage was sanctioned. This was bad enough, but by now Philip was convinced Gilbert would never have actually married

Rose once he had bedded her. Unlike her, he knew just how adverse to the idea of marriage his stepbrother really was. It had all been a ruse to get his way with her, nothing more. The fact that he had not allowed her to justify herself was proof enough that he had been only too happy to dispose of her while he could and had never meant to marry her.

Even Philip, who had come to expect nothing from his stepbrother, had been shocked to see him sink so low.

He did not tell Rose what he suspected, however. She was ashamed enough of having agreed to his demands. It would be cruel to make her see that she would have sacrificed her dignity in vain.

"Gilbert never forgave me for exposing his true nature to our father, but then, it is not as if we had been close before, so I did not lose much."

Rose emptied her cup of ale with the air of someone bracing herself for her next comment.

"Do you have any children?" she surprised him by asking.

While they were talking openly Rose seized the opportunity to ask Philip the question that had bothered her all day long. She had noted his manner with Edward earlier, how he had instinctively known how to carry him, how he had made him laugh. His whole attitude had borne the hallmark of a man at ease with children, used to dealing with them. She knew he was not married, but he could have many by-blows. Not for a moment did she imagine a man like him led a celibate life. The very reason he had ended up in her bed at Harleith Castle was that he had thought to go to one of his conquests. She did not doubt the list of women who had enjoyed his favors would be impressive.

Besides, his reaction when they had met that day on the beach had made her think that it was not the first time a woman had come to him claiming to be carrying his child. It had been almost as if he had expected her to say so.

"I had a child. A little girl," he said, his face clouded with sadness. "She died last year."

Died…

Rose's hand flew to her chest. "Oh, God, I'm so sorry."

Instantly she berated herself for having asked the question and reawakened the pain of his loss. Feeling cold to the bottom of her soul, she looked at Philip's somber expression. How could anyone bear the agony of losing a child? Henry's death had been a dreadful blow, but it was not the same, he was not the flesh of her flesh. Having Edward taken away from her had been heart-wrenching, but at least he wasn't dead.

What Philip had endured was worse than everything she could imagine.

"Emma was seven years old when she died. A fever…" He did not elaborate. There was no need. So many children did not live to see their tenth birthday…

Rose wanted to ask about the girl's mother and why Philip had not married her. He had been so prompt to protect her reputation and ask for her hand when he had thought her with child that she could not imagine him acting any differently with Emma's mother. But perhaps there had been a good reason behind it. Perhaps the woman had already been married or had died in childbirth.

Despite her curiosity, she stayed silent. The last thing she wanted was to make another blunder and force him to relive the tragedy.

“Her mother, Hettie, never allowed me to marry her, arguing that she was not a suitable wife for me and, undeniably, people would have agreed with her,” he explained, tilting his head to her.

Rose blushed in embarrassment. Evidently her curiosity must have shown on her face.

“Why is that?” she whispered. If he had guessed that she was dying to ask questions, she might as well do so.

“She was only a maid at Harleith Castle. She was relieved by my reaction when she told me about the babe but absolutely refused to hear about the lord of the castle’s son making a laughingstock of himself by marrying her. Gilbert, of course, argued that she was the only wife I was fit for having.” Philip gave a snort. “I provided for her well and she lived at the castle for a couple of years with Emma.”

“Do you still see Hettie now?” she asked, although she had already guessed the answer. Without needing confirmation, she knew that the woman she had seen the other day at Wicklow Castle wrapped in his arms was none other than the mother of his child. There had been more affection in their embrace than lust. It warmed her to know that he had not written the poor woman out of his life now that their illegitimate child had died and he had become a powerful lord.

“Yes, often. She married a good man from the village five years ago and settled there with Emma,” he explained. “While I would have preferred to keep my daughter with me, I did not have the heart to separate her from her mother. I told you, I believe young children should be with their mother whenever possible. As soon as Emma had gone, I left Harleith Castle. I would have gone much earlier had I not had her to take care of."

Emotion swelled within Rose.

Everything she had heard about Philip tonight, everything he had done since they had met, pointed to a selfless, thoughtful, honorable, and dependable man. This man could have been her husband—he could have been the one taking care of her and her son. She suspected that no one would suit the task better.

With him she felt alive, something she had not felt since Henry's death, and she could not ignore the desire he stirred within her any longer, no matter how many cups of ale she emptied.

She watched his long, elegant fingers wrapped around his own cup, and a shiver ran down her spine. Thankfully, Philip never behaved in her presence as if they had shared a bed together, as if she already knew what his caresses felt like, as if he had brushed his lips over her skin in fiery kisses. He never alluded to the fact that he had praised her body, licked her breasts, stroked her intimately, made her moan like a wanton and even cry out when an excess of pleasure had washed over her.

But she could not forget any of it. In fact…

She wanted to experience it again.

"It's very late," she murmured. Through the window, nothing could be seen. Night had truly set in. Philip could not leave now, it would not be safe travel for a man on his own, even one as formidable as he was. "Will you sleep here tonight?" she asked, sounding breathless.

"Rose." The use of her name made her all warm inside. When she finally dared to look at him, the warmth became a blazing hot fire. "If I stay here, I am not at all sure I will sleep," he finished with a growl.

"Nor will I," she answered in the same tone. No. She would not sleep.

Or at least, not alone.

Rose could have told herself she was grateful for what he had done, that her mind was addled, her judgment altered by today's unexpected events, but she did not want to lie to herself thus. She was grateful, of course, more than she had ever been in her life, but the truth was she wanted Philip to make love to her more than anything else in the world. In this moment, he wasn't the man who had given her son back to her—he was the lover who had inflamed her body and who was looking at her with fiery eyes, ready to take her to bed.

She heard herself gasp in anticipation of his touch.

Philip knew he had to leave now or he would kiss Rose and then take her to bed. He wanted to, desperately, but it would not be fair to her. It would be playing on the gratefulness she felt toward him, something he was loath to do. Reining in his urges out of consideration for a woman's feelings was a new experience for him. Not that he usually ignored their qualms, far from it, but rather he set about trying to make them overcome them, with resounding success.

But in front of Rose he was helpless.

He could not bring himself to cause her a moment's distress. He did not want to take advantage of her moment of vulnerability. After the emotional day she'd had, she would not be feeling herself, and he did not want a woman to come to him simply because she was grateful and felt she owed it to him for what he had done. She had allowed him to possess her when she did not truly want him, and he could not bear to do the same again.

However he could not deny he had wanted her every

moment of that day, from the moment she had stood in front of him in that serviceable dress to when she had looked up at him with wide eyes with longing just a moment ago. Everything she was, everything she did appealed to him. When she had climbed atop her horse and revealed her leg, he had almost reached out to kiss it. When she had faced Baron Chichester with aplomb, he had cheered inwardly. When she had embraced her son with such love, he had almost wrapped his arms around them both.

Every single moment of that day had been exquisite torture. He had been hard for longer than he could remember. At the first touch he would explode.

He took a step back.

"Rose, I have to go," he breathed, as his body became unbearably taut at the idea of taking her into his arms.

"No, you do not," she murmured back.

She walked closer to him, so close that her smell hit him. He gave a mental curse, feeling himself grow even harder. If she touched him he would not stand a chance. Any scruples, any doubts he might have, everything would vanish, and he would be lost.

He took another two steps back, but she only smiled and followed him.

"Are you afraid of me, my lord?" she murmured. "I wouldn't have thought that one lone woman would be enough to frighten a warrior like you."

Rose inhaled at her daring. Since when did she go around provoking men and making lewd propositions to them? But her body was pulsing so hard with need that she could not behave otherwise. If Philip was not going to come to her of his own free will, she would have to make him come.

But how? She was not well versed in the art of seduction. How did a woman go about enticing a man she desired? With Henry it had been simple—she had let herself be seduced. Now she was supposed to take the initiative.

She bit her lip in dismay.

It was when Rose licked her lips that Philip realized that she wanted him as strongly as he wanted her. Not because she was not thinking straight, but because she was just as haunted by the memory of their night together as he was. She wanted him, not as the savior who had given her her son back but as a man, as a lover who would make her melt in pleasure.

He allowed the last of his hesitations to recede to the back of his mind. If she wanted him, then he did not need to feel bad about taking her. Right now they were just a man and a woman who desired each other. Nothing else mattered.

But as much as she wanted him, he knew Rose would not take the first step. If she thought herself capable of doing it, she would already have done it. But at the last moment her feminine modesty had prevailed. All her life she would have been told that it was not a woman's place to initiate lovemaking, that it was unseemly. As the man, he would have to be the one in charge.

And he had no qualms about it.

Without further ado he wrapped his arms around her waist and brought their two bodies into close contact, so close that his hardness pressed against her stomach. The warm softness of it sent shards of longing up his spine. God help him, he would need iron control not to rush this and give her as much pleasure as he had on their night together. The memory of the cry of surrender she had given inflamed him further, making him stiffen almost to the point of pain.

"No, I'm not afraid of you, Rose. And one lone woman is just what I need right now."

Now that he knew who he was holding in his arms, he would enjoy making love to her even more. That first night he had imagined her to be the insignificant Lady Hershey, yet he had been blown away by their connection, and the intensity of his pleasure. Now that he knew Rose for a brave, caring, strong woman, he could not wait to possess her again, all the while looking deep into her eyes.

Remembering how she had tricked him did not dampen his ardor, rather the contrary. A woman so selfless and determined would make for a passionate lover. She moved, the gesture making her stomach muscles ripple against his manhood.

He growled. "Are you sure you want this?" he asked, holding on to the last shred of sanity.

She did not answer, but she smiled and lifted her face to him in readiness for his kiss. He took her mouth, unable to keep his desire in check a moment longer. He had not kissed her before, at least not whilst knowing who she was, and she had been passive, even wary at first. This time she kissed him back, with such passion that he feared he would end up hurting her.

His tongue licked along her bottom lip, tasting her. There was a hint of spice there.

The Lord help him, he was going to lose his mind and frighten her.

Then she surprised him by running her hands along

his spine and landing her hands on his buttocks to draw him closer to her, the message crystal clear.

"No!" He disentangled himself from her embrace swiftly, feeling on the verge of losing his mind. Another moment and he would sit her on the table and take her where they were and risk people walking in on them. He did not want to do that, and he did not want to rush this. "Not here," he panted, speaking against her lips. "Not like this. I need to see you, I need to *hear* you. Take me to your room, Rose."

She didn't hesitate.

Rose knew that anyone crossing their path would guess where they were going and why. Her cheeks were flushed, her lips swollen from their kiss, and as for Philip, well… There would be no ignoring the bulge at the front of his hose, which looked about to burst at the seams. Her cheeks flushed deeper. Though mercifully it was not as visible, she was just as aroused as he was. Behind her she could sense his masculine presence, and her whole body started to burn in anticipation.

He was right to want to go somewhere private. This night would be something to remember. She didn't want anything to compromise it. This time she would not be wary of his touch, she would revel in it.

They soon reached her room. She walked in first, making sure no one was around to see them, then Philip followed suit. Rose heard him close the door behind him, but she did not turn around. She let him come to her.

Neither of them said a word for a long moment. Then two hands landed on her hips, the contact making her skin prickle and burn. She gave a moan that ended in a sigh of pure longing.

"You want me." It was not a question.

"Yes."

She leaned back into him until the back of her head was resting against his chest. One of Philip's hands travelled upward and came to cup her breast while the other crept downward and stopped only when it had reached the spot between her legs. The position was so suggestive, he had taken possession of her body with such breathtaking assurance that she moaned. How was she going to survive this? She let out a shuddering breath, and the hand at her breast came to lift her chin. He turned her head to him and gave her a scorching kiss. At the same time the fingers cupping her intimately started a teasing dance.

Rose feared she would explode in longing and kissed him with all the passion she was capable of. It would not be long before she needed more, as exquisite as his caresses were. It took all her willpower not to beg him to take her to bed now. He was as ready as she was—she could feel the hard proof of it against the small of her back.

Her clothes disappeared without her quite understanding how he had done it. All the while he kept stroking her, teasing her, kissing her. His own clothes were discarded just as mysteriously. They were now both standing naked in front of each other, trembling with the intensity of their need. Still, she took her time to look at him, all parts of him. She had only ever seen his chest before, that night at Harleith Castle when she'd had no idea who he was. It had blown her away even when she'd thought she hated him. Now that she allowed herself to revel in his beauty, she saw his chiseled torso for the marvel it really was.

And the rest of him was just as magnificent.

His limbs were long and lean, corded with muscles. His skin was a rich amber color, so much so that she briefly wondered if he didn't have Mediterranean ancestry. His dark eyes, which appealed to her so, certainly made that a possibility.

What would he think of her, she wondered suddenly?

He must have seen countless women naked, and she lacked any exotic appeal. She looked just like any other English lady, and one who was not in the first flush of youth and had borne a child already.

She fought the urge to cover herself, guessing he would only order her to take her hands away if she did. Besides, all she could see in his face was admiration. Could it be that she pleased him just the way she was? She remained in front of him, her breathing fast, her heart thudding in anticipation.

Finally, he was seeing Rose naked. He had made love to her in the dark, and when she had faced him that night in Harleith Castle she had been dressed in her mantle. He had guessed then that her body would be glorious, and it was. The perfect breasts crowned with amber-colored nipples, the flared hips and narrow waist, the creamy skin… Dear God, it was enough to make his mouth water. This woman was made to be stroked, suckled, and kissed from head to toe. And he would do just that.

Tonight he would take his time and savor every inch of her, swallow her every breath, enjoy her every moan.

This time Rose decided she would allow herself the pleasure of bedding Philip without the hindrance of thinking he was a man she despised.

Although he had already possessed her body, he had

done so under a misunderstanding, and she needed the satisfaction of knowing he was a man she had chosen willingly, a man she wanted. And, just as importantly, she wanted him to make love to her as Rose, not by mistake, not because he thought she was Lady Hershey or anyone else, but because he wanted *her*.

Just as if he'd guessed her need, he looked her straight in the eye and called out her name softly.

"Rose. Tonight I will know who I am holding in my arms. Come here," he said in a low, hungry growl. There was no doubting his longing for her. She had wanted to see the desire he felt for her, to see that he was attracted to her, and his words, along with the urgency in his voice, had done just that.

Moved by a desire just as strong, she pressed herself against him.

Rose gave a little cry of surprise when Philip placed his hands underneath her thighs and lifted her abruptly off her feet. Automatically she closed her arms around his neck and wrapped her legs around his waist for support. In that shocking position their eyes were level. She saw the liquid gold center of his irises, and she melted.

With a measure of shock, delicious shock, she felt the tip of his manhood slide into her. Her eyes widened at the same time as her body softened to accommodate him. She had never imagined a man could do something like that. Henry had never taken her anywhere other than in their bed. She doubted he would have done such a wild thing as making love to her whilst standing up, even supposing he had been strong enough to do it. Thank God Philip was both strong and wild enough, for the feeling was heavenly. She inhaled sharply and tightened her hold around him while he sank deeper into her quivering flesh.

"Oh!" she whimpered, feeling on the brink of release already.

Philip lifted her slightly and plunged back inside of her, deeper than before. There he stayed for a moment. Then, without breaking the contact between them, he brought her over to the bed and came to lie on top of her. The last time he had made love to her, it had been pitch black and she had kept her eyes tightly shut throughout. There had been no chance of taking the slightest glimpse of him. Today, however, she reveled in the sight of Philip poised over her. The muscles on his shoulders and neck were bulging with the effort it took him to hold his weight off her. The gleam in his eyes was incendiary, and the curve on his lips full of sensual promise.

She lifted her legs and locked her ankles behind his back, drawing him as close as she could to her. When at last he moved, she closed her fingers on his buttocks and arched her back.

Oh, God.

"Yes," he grunted, flexing his muscles as he plunged inside her again and again. The relentless rhythm stoked her need to an almost unbearable pitch. She whimpered. How was she going to survive this?

Nothing had prepared Philip for such pleasure. He felt like a youth bedding his very first conquest, overawed and grateful. Rose was squeezing him like a fist, scalding him in her liquid heat, coaxing his release.

"Yes. Just like that, Rose," he grunted. "Take me. Take all of me."

Blinding light exploded behind Rose's eyelids, and the world dimmed for a moment.

****

Dawn was graying in the horizon.

Rose's eyes fluttered open. Immediately her hand found its way to Philip's chest. Under her fingers, the smooth skin was calling out for caresses. Wonderingly, she let her hand follow a path across one pectoral to the other one, then down to his stomach. His body was possibly the softest thing she had ever touched. How could a man so strong feel so delicate? The honeyed skin was like silk. She grazed her knuckles on the trail of hair starting at his navel.

Suddenly a big hand clamped down over hers.

"Whatever it is you are doing, my lady, keep doing it," Philip purred in her ear. "Move the sheet if it is in the way."

Rose reddened, not because she felt caught out but because she was sorely tempted to take him at his word. Could she dare to do it? Before releasing her hand Philip planted a kiss on the center of her palm. Encouraged by this mark of tenderness, she carried on with her exploration. Yes, she would dare. The sheet was kicked away, and she resumed her caresses, all the while looking him in the eye. As she got lower, the downy fuzz on his stomach gave way to rougher hair. She gulped when her knuckles brushed against the tip of his manhood. He was hard, already aroused and ready for her.

Just as she was for him.

The moment was unbearably erotic. Feeling that she was the one in charge only added to the frisson. Finally she dared to take a look at his lower body. Oh, my. Rose paused, biting her bottom lip in hesitation. It was one thing wanting to do something, quite another actually doing it.

“Don’t feel you have to stop now,” he murmured softly, nudging at her cheek with the tip of his nose. The gesture was surprisingly playful and tender.

“I don’t know where to start,” she said, almost to herself.

“Here, I think.”

He took her hand and placed it on his erection. Her fingers closed around the thick shaft, feeling it pulse under her touch. It was warm, and surprisingly smooth. Her hand slid lower and she heard a hiss in her ear. Encouraged, she did it again.

“It doesn’t feel as I imagined it would,” Rose said in a breath. “I never…”

The enormity of what she was doing hit her almost like a physical blow. She was in a bed with a man who was not her husband, and her hand was closed around his… She covered her mouth in embarrassment. She had been about to do what she had never dared to do—or even considered doing—to the man she had married for love. The man next to her might look like an angel, but he was not Henry, her Henry, the father of her child, the man who had wed her in defiance of his own family. Surely she owed her husband more loyalty than this?

Surely she should not be here, stroking another man and allowing him to pleasure her as intimately as Philip had?

A garbled cry escaped her lips when she remembered what he had done to her last night. He had kissed every inch of her body with relish. Every part of her, even the most secret. She had screwed her eyes shut at the time, for fear the sight would either send her mad with shame or make her explode with lust. Even more worryingly than that, she had feared that the lewd image of Philip's dark head buried between her thighs would haunt her for the rest of her life. It had all been in vain. If she did not know what it looked like to have a man kissing your female core, she certainly would not forget what it *felt* like.

The memory would stay with her forever, and make her go crazy with longing.

And now she had almost done the same to him!

Letting go of Philip's manhood, Rose recoiled to the far end of the bed as quickly as if his body had been made of metal in fusion.

"I'm sorry, I cannot do this. I don't know how I could… You must go, please."

She retreated as far as she could but did not leave the bed. She was still naked, and all she could do was clutch the sheet to her chest compulsively. Last night she had pursued him, teased him, asked him if he was afraid of her, for heaven's sake! How could she have forgotten herself thus?

Seeing Rose cover herself in shame, Philip sighed and mentally cursed his inability to resist her teasing. He should never have suggested that she stroke him so intimately. It had been too much. She was not ready for such caresses. It was already a miracle she had given in to her desire for him the evening before. He should not have asked for more. He had stayed awake long into the night wondering how, come morning, she would handle the fact that she had been unfaithful to her beloved husband. Of course, this was not what had really happened, for Henry Maltravers was dead. You could not be unfaithful to a dead man, but he suspected that Rose would see it that way. She had only ever bedded one other person in her life, a man she loved.

At the very least, she would see what had happened as a betrayal of his memory.

And he had been right.

"Listen, Rose, if you want me to leave, of course I will. But please do not spend the rest of your life torturing yourself about what happened last night. We both wanted it. Your husband is not here anymore," he said as gently as he could. "You have not been unfaithful to him. If he loved you, as you told me he did, then I know he would not want you to punish yourself for surrendering to the desire you felt for another man when he is not here to attend to your needs anymore."

"How do you know what he would have liked?" Rose spat. How could he be so presumptuous as to tell her what she should feel, what Henry would think if he saw her opening her legs for another man? A fresh burst of shame washed through her. He would most certainly *not* congratulate her for behaving like a wanton! "You never met him."

"No. But I know that he defied his family for the love he bore you, that he married you despite what his father thought of you. That is the mark of a good man," Philip said firmly. "And a good man would not want his widow to keep on punishing herself for something she wanted to do. He would not want her to stop living because he is dead."

A long wail escaped her throat. Why was Philip being so reasonable, yet so cruel at the same time? She did not want to listen to this, not right now, not while his heat was warming the bed next to her, the bed she had once shared with Henry.

"Please, just leave, I cannot…" She was on the verge

of panic.

Thankfully he got up without comment.

She averted her eyes, unable to bear seeing him naked right now. The rustle of fabric while he got dressed was excruciating, for even if she could not see anything she could not help but picture the glorious body he was covering up. Eventually she turned and watched him put his boots on. When he straightened up, restored to his usual magnificence, she could not repress a gasp. The man facing her now was undoubtedly Lord Chrystenden. There was little evidence of Philip, the fiery lover who had held her in his arms the night before.

He watched her with an undecipherable expression on his face, when only the day before his whole being had been ablaze with desire for her. The hazel eyes were almost cold, no longer burning with longing, his stance stiff. There was nothing in common between this man and the one who had taken her to bed and whispered terms of endearment in her ear, asking her to spread her legs for him. It did not make it any easier for her to face him.

If he was now too remote to be any real threat to her senses, he was also a hundred times more intimidating.

She steeled herself for the task of dismissing him because deep down she knew he had done nothing wrong. *She* was the one at fault. Why should he be the one under accusation, the one having to flee? It didn't seem fair. Still, he had to go, because in spite of everything, she did not trust herself not to tumble into bed with him again. This, more than anything else, was what horrified her. Why did he have such a pull on her? Why was she so weak?

Why could she not write him out of her life?

It would have to be the last time she and Philip ever met—that was the only solution. Whatever she felt about him, Rose could not bear the idea that the next time they met she would want him again. It had happened every time she had found herself face to face with him. As much as she told herself she should not think thus, she could not deny the appeal he exerted over her. He was far too handsome, far too magnetic, far too dangerous for her peace of mind.

She should have resented him for making her feel so wretched, but she could not. Instead she hated herself for allowing her senses to rule over her head. Philip was a kind man, a model of generosity. He was not the one owing his loyalty to a dead husband. He had no reason to resist the attraction between them.

What he had done for her and Edward was the best thing anyone had ever done for her, but it did not make what *she* had done any less of a betrayal.

"I want you to leave and never come back," she whispered. "There can be little we have to say to each other."

He twisted his lips, the lips she had kissed so passionately the night before, and she flushed when she remembered that they had done a lot more than talk the night before. She carried on before he could say anything.

"Your conscience is clear. You have permitted my son and me to be reunited, and I will forever be grateful to you for this, but I cannot bear to think that I allowed myself to…" She closed her eyes in mortification. "I know you did not force me, and it only makes me more ashamed of myself."

"Don't be. Please. If it is any consolation, no one

will know what happened last night."

She hesitated, and almost thanked him. Once again he was behaving as honorably as she could have hoped.

Moments ago, they had been lying in bed together, naked, waking up from a night of unbridled passion, and she had been stroking him sensually. Then all of a sudden she was ordering him to leave. In the circumstances, a man might be forgiven for showing a bit of temper, if not demand that she finish what she had started… But not only had Philip obeyed her without a word but he also seemed to understand the reasons behind her reaction and sympathize with them. And now he was reassuring her, telling her she had nothing to worry about…

It was hard to make sense of it.

"Why are you being so fair? So reasonable with me?" she whimpered, feeling she did not deserve his generosity.

He had always treated her in a respectful manner, except perhaps on the morning of their wedding when he had discovered she had lied to him. Then he had been harsh toward her, but this reaction was to be expected, even justified, given the circumstances. He had just found out she had lied about carrying his child so she could marry him for his money, or so he had thought.

Philip gave an amused snort at her question. "Why am I being fair? Because, in case it had escaped your notice, Rose, I consider myself a fair and reasonable man. I can see why you did everything you did with my stepbrother and me to ensure you would get your son back. I understand how you must feel about having allowed me to do to you what no man other than your husband has ever done to you." He branded her with a searing look. “And more.”

Rose gulped and clenched her legs tight in reaction to his words. How had he guessed that Henry had never dared to pleasure her in the shocking manner he had, with his mouth? Then she reflected that her reaction must have made it clear. A lover as skilled as Philip would have guessed that she had never experienced anything like it. He would have seen that she was shocked by the newness of it all and by the intensity of her pleasure. The memory of his tongue darting between her thighs made her hide her face in her hands.

“If you truly understand how I feel, then you will stop reminding me of what we did,” she said in a deathly whisper.

Whatever he was saying, she knew she would spend the rest of her days torturing herself over what had happened. She would never be able to forgive herself, not so much for allowing another man to make love to her but for all but forcing him to do it. Left to his own devices, Philip would have found the strength to fight his desire for her. But she had wanted him so badly that she had actually been the one initiating their lovemaking.

It had been an irrepressible force, but that didn’t excuse anything. She should have been stronger.

Philip stepped over to where she was still sitting, clutching at her sheet spasmodically. One finger came under her chin to raise it. She wanted to turn her head to the side but she could not.

“Rose, please. Listen to me.”

She would never know what he meant to say to her, for at that precise moment there was a knock on the door. She gave a muffled cry. Oh, no, not now! No one should be allowed to suspect the presence of a man in her bedchamber! She would never live down the shame.

"What is it?" she asked, doing her best not to betray her panic. Was the door locked?

"Master Edward is up and has expressed a wish to see you."

Rose recognized the voice of the village girl Philip had insisted on hiring to help around the house now that Edward was to live with her again.

"Tell him I will be down presently. I will need to get dressed."

Dear God, her son wanted her and she was still naked in bed, with a man who was not his father in her room. How much more mortifying could the situation be?

"Please, you need to leave," she whispered, looking at Philip with pleading eyes.

He shook his head. "Not right now."

Rose's heart gave a jolt.

What did he mean? Perhaps he still wanted her and would not leave until he had obtained satisfaction. She swallowed hard. It was possible. After all, only a moment ago she had been on the verge of pleasuring him, and they both knew that he had not initiated it. He might feel frustrated and want to see her finish what she had so boldly started. Nervously she stole a glance toward his hose, not a difficult thing to do when he was standing uncomfortably close to her.

Philip gave a tight smile when he saw where Rose was looking. Mercifully, getting dressed had helped in subduing the desire raging in his body. He was not hard anymore, but… If she carried on looking at him while her mouth was level with his crotch, it might not last long.

"It's nothing like that," he said in a low voice, moving away from her. With her naked shoulders exposed and her hair cascading down her back, she was just too tempting. "You will be pleased to know that I have some self-control, though I have to admit you make it particularly taxing, in your current state." He gritted his teeth. Indeed. "But I told you, I am a reasonable man."

She gave a sigh of relief, as if for a moment she had feared he was a lusty beast that would not be controlled.

"Still, you must go."

"Not now, when I might be seen coming out of your bedchamber. I shall have to wait here a moment and slip out after you've gone." Philip looked around the room in one all-encompassing glance and frowned. That was all very well, but there was nowhere for him to hide when Rose's lady came to dress her. "Your maid, though, will see me when she comes. You might have to make up an excuse to refuse her help."

Rose had to tell him the truth, however surprising he might find it. "There is no need. I always get dressed by myself."

Although usually I am alone when I do it.

"I see." There was something like laughter in his voice. He would be thinking back to the way she had refused Emeline as a lady-in-waiting. "Dare I offer my assistance if this is the case?"

"No, thank you. But you could perhaps…"

"Avert my eyes?" he finished in her stead. "I could. Not that I have not seen you naked before."

Oh, he had done much more than *see* her! She reddened. Why did he have to remind her of the fact?

"Please. Could you just turn around?"

Before she had finished her sentence, Philip had turned to face the opposite wall. Feeling very self-conscious, Rose got up and shrugged her shift on, all the while keeping her eye on Philip to see if he was true to his word. He did not move so much as a muscle. Reassured, she reached out for her gown and started to put it on.

Philip watched Rose arch her back to lift the heavy mass of her hair out of her shift. Then she stepped into the gown, lifted it up, and slipped her arms into the sleeves. He could tell she had not lied, she was used to getting dressed by herself. Her gestures were swift, assured.

Arousing as hell.

It had not been deliberate, but as he turned around he had found himself staring at a reflection of Rose in the glass panel of the window. The image was blurred, but it was enough to allow his imagination to supply beyond what he could only glimpse, and he had made no effort to avert his eyes.

His manhood surged back to life. This time there would be no coaxing it down, not while he watched her dress and imagined the smooth, white body under the clothes. Still, he could not look away.

He had held this desirable woman in his arms the previous night, made love to her with as much passion as he had ever done, and she had answered with equal spontaneity. Even more significantly, they had shared a moment of unexpected intimacy beforehand, when she had thanked him for restoring her son to her and he had talked about Hettie and his little girl, something he rarely did. Maybe that was what had made their lovemaking so satisfying. It had felt more meaningful than a simple joining of bodies. There had been a deeper connection, something he had never experienced with anyone else, something he could not quite account for, something that deserved to be investigated further.

But now he would not be given the chance. Rose wanted him not only out of her bedchamber but out of her life, and all because she was ashamed of having made love to him, of having felt desire and acted on it. The idea did not sit well with him. No one should ever feel guilty for something like that, something that was as natural as breathing. Neither of them were betrothed or married. They were both free to be with each other. There was no shame in what they had done, and Rose should not punish herself for it.

If only he could make her understand…

Briefly he wondered if he should marry her after all. Now that he knew why she had lied to him, he understood that she had not set out to trap him. Rose was not the cynical manipulator he had taken her for—far from it. She had not tried to marry him or his stepbrother for vile, opportunistic reasons, to gain a prestigious title or to have access to their fortune, but to ensure a little boy would not grow up without his loving mother.

The way she had behaved with Edward had affected him deeply. She had so much love to give, and she was not afraid to show it, even in front of people who disapproved of her manners. He had to admire her for that. So many people hid their inner feelings, tried to conform to what was expected, or simply were too afraid to be themselves. Not Rose. She had been overjoyed to see her son, and she had not let anything or anyone spoil the moment.

And then she had thanked him with such earnest

emotion that he had felt his heart melt in his chest. Up until then, she had stirred his body, but she had not really provoked anything deeper inside him than a desire to take her to bed.

Last night it had all been different.

Which of course did not excuse his weakness. Instead of getting overwhelmed by his desire for her, he should have understood that she was only looking at him with desire because of what he had done for her son. He should have waited, certain as he had been that in the morning she would have sobered and regret giving in to her desire.

But he had been unable to be the fair and reasonable man he prided himself on being. Once again he had acted on impulse.

Whatever her reasons for wanting him, for that fleeting moment Rose *had* wanted him, and, sensible as he was, he was also a man. The need to make love to her had washed over him, sweeping away everything in his path.

Even now he could not regret it. She had surrendered to his most daring caresses in a moving way, and he feared that from now on he would never be satisfied with less than this total surrender when bedding a woman. Making love to someone who was overawed by the sensations wrenched out of her, who gave herself without reservations, was like nothing he had ever experienced.

"I am dressed. You may turn around."

Rose's voice reached him from the other end of the room. Philip's lips twisted. He already knew she was ready, as he had just watched her smooth the skirts down the length of her thighs in the blurry windowpane.

“Why do you not have a lady to help you dress?” he asked in an effort to distract his mind, or rather another part of his anatomy, from the memory of his own hands skimming the length of her thighs. The moans he had got in response had been the most exquisite sound he had ever heard.

“I do not have the means to pay one, that’s why.”

Rose had guessed Philip would be surprised at her lack of help. It was far from common for a lady not to employ ladies-in-waiting or maids, and she needed to explain herself. She could have said she had been raised without one, but she did not want to lie to him.

“Last year when Baron Chichester started to threaten to take Edward away, I sent a lot of my people away so I did not have to pay their wages anymore. I wanted to save as much money as I could to show him I still had the means to raise my son properly.”

Philip nodded, remembering the old mare in her stables, the state of the manor house. How had he not thought of it before? Without her pension and her husband’s family’s help, she would have struggled to make ends meet.

“But it wasn’t enough,” he said softly.

“No. I quickly came to the conclusion that I would never be able to provide Edward with the comfort he was entitled to, and of course Baron Chichester did as well. I would never have been able to get him a pony or afford to pay for proper tuition.” She wrung her hands together and lowered her head in what appeared to be embarrassment. He could not countenance it.

“There is no need to be ashamed. This selflessness does you credit,” he said through gritted teeth. She had sacrificed much for her son, and all in vain. Once again she was feeling guilty for something that should make her proud. “You placed your son’s needs above your own. It is the mark of a loving mother.”

“In any case, I do not need a lady-in-waiting. Lots of women manage without one. I told you I was not as high born as Henry, and it is not so difficult to dress oneself if simple gowns are chosen.” She gestured at the one she was wearing right now.

True, the cut was simple and it lacked the embellishments fashionable ladies favored, but all the same no one would have thought anything was lacking. The luscious body underneath helped set it off to perfection. The loveliness of her face alone made you forget you were not looking at a princess in her best court dress. Rose in a plain woolen dress was worth ten Lady Hersheys clad in satin.

“Indeed,” he murmured, coming to her. “There is, however, an unsightly crease here at the back. If you will allow me…”

He reached out to rearrange the folds of her bodice. Immediately Rose’s heartbeat started to go wild. She could usually dress herself with reasonable efficiency, but today she had been so unsettled by Philip’s presence, so disturbed by the memory of their night together, that she had not managed it half as well as she could have. It was no surprise he should find her inadequately attired.

To see Philip, without doubt the most masculine man she had ever set eyes on, arrange the folds of her plain gown as carefully as if it had been made of silk and her in danger of breaking at the slightest touch made her shiver from head to toe. It gave her a sudden, irrepressible craving. She wanted this man to be the one to take care of her and Edward. He would do a splendid job of it, he had proven it a hundredfold, in grand gestures and minute detail.

What's more, she didn't want to be alone anymore. She wanted him to be by her side constantly, in her bed.

In her life.

The way he was looking after her, the care he had taken when riding with Edward in front of him, the tenderness in his voice when he had talked about his little girl, everything told her that this man was a protector to his core, the man she needed to get over her grief, to bring some much-needed order to her life and warmth to her soul.

She could not dwell on the notion, however. It would only make her long for something she had no right to.

"There," he said, smoothing his hand along her back in a loving gesture. "Perfect. Now you can go."

"What will you do?" she asked, utterly undone by such tenderness. The fiery lover had been replaced by an infinitely more dangerous man, a man who made her long for far more than nights of unbridled passion.

"I will wait until it is safe for me to leave the room, and then I'll go. No one will know I spent the night here, I swear."

"But your horse…"

"Christ, yes, of course, my horse!" He frowned. Once again his levelheaded self had been defeated by the woman in front of him. "That is a problem." If no one had to know that he had gone to Rose's bed, with his stallion in the stables, there would be no ignoring the fact that he had spent the night in the house. Where would they claim he had slept?

"With your permission, I will say that you found a

woman at the village and stayed to spend the night with her," Rose said in a breath. "If no one sees you leaving my room, it might work."

It was a ridiculous explanation, but her addled mind could not present her with a better suggestion. One thing played in her favor. No one would ever imagine that she, the supposedly respectable widow, had been the woman in question. Not only had she not been seen receiving any man since Henry's death, but who would think she possessed the appeal needed to attract a man like Lord Chrystenden?

"I don't know if I care for this explanation, which presents me as an indefatigable womanizer, jumping at the opportunity to bed women wherever I go, but I guess there is little choice." Philip's lips quivered, and she could tell he was fighting a smile.

Oh, God.

Rose whimpered. How could a man be so irresistible? She was about to collapse under the strain of trying not to fall into his arms. He had to leave, now, or she would not resist temptation. Before she could stop him, he placed a kiss on her lips, a light, intimate kiss that somehow burned its way into her soul.

"Thank you," he said, pressing his forehead against hers. Rose's eyes widened in astonishment and her chest constricted in emotion at the same time. Why on earth was he thanking her?

"I should be the one thanking you, after what you did for me," she said in a breath.

"This has nothing to do with Edward, though I will not deny it did me good to hold a child in my arms again. I had not realized how much I was missing it."

The tightening in her chest became almost

unbearable. “So why are you thanking me?”

“I made love to you four months ago, and I know you enjoyed it,” he purred into her ear. Rose blushed. He was referring to the way she had melted under his touch despite herself and cried out in pleasure. “But I needed to know that I bedded you at least once with your full consent, because you wanted me, not anyone else. I needed to know that I had come to you in desire, not by mistake. Now it is done at last.”

Every word was like a dagger into Rose’s heart. What could she say after such a declaration? Why was he making it so hard for her to hold on to her dignity, to walk away from him?

She should be ashamed, but how could she be ashamed in the presence of a man who had seen her naked and then helped her dress? She should be angry, but how could she be angry with someone who was so honest with her? But she needed to be! If she wasn’t furious, if she didn’t feel guilty, how could she justify sending him away?

How could she bear to see him leave?

“Go, Rose. Go to your son,” he murmured, pushing her to the door as if he knew she was rooted to the spot by too many conflicting emotions and needed help in taking a decision. “I will see myself out. You need never see me again, if that is what you wish.”

She hesitated. Was it what she wanted?

It was certainly the safest, most honorable course of action, but was that what she really wanted? Was she strong enough to do it?

These questions would have to wait for another time. Edward was expecting her. For months she had wanted just that, to wake up and go to her son. So what was she waiting for?

She left the room without a backward glance.

Philip sat on the bed and rubbed his hand over his face.

What had happened the day before should have left him satisfied and finally at peace with himself. After her shocking revelation on their supposed wedding day, he had sworn to help Rose get her son back, and he had done so. He had resolved to convince the king to restore her allowance, and he had succeeded in doing so. He had wanted to repair the wrong he had caused her, first by bedding her by mistake, then by accusing her of vile scheming. He had needed to go to her bed as a lover she desired.

Now he had done all that, and more, with unmitigated success. He was finally free of the guilt he had been carrying. He should have been able to put the whole adventure behind him and move on.

So why was he feeling so wretched? Why was he feeling as if everything was merely about to start? He had been so convinced that once everything was back in order he would be content!

He was far from content. An uncomfortable feeling was gnawing at him, and he started to suspect he would never be content unless he kept Rose by his side.

Chapter 10

In the end, they did see each other again.

As Philip was tightening the girth on his stallion's saddle, he heard the patter of tiny feet on the dusty ground. He turned in time to see Edward running toward him, followed by his smiling mother.

"Good morning, Master Edward," he greeted, relieved to see that Rose's good mood had been restored since she had left the bedchamber. "I trust you slept well?"

The little boy ignored the question completely. His eyes were riveted on the horse. "How old is he?" he asked, eyeing him up with envy.

"A little over five years old."

"Beautiful!" The blue eyes almost popped out of their sockets.

Philip smiled at the enthusiasm and ruffled the boy's hair. "Yes, he is."

"What's his name?"

"Edward, I'm sure his lordship is eager to leave," Rose interrupted, placing a hand on her son's shoulder. "We are keeping him from important business. Now, run to the kitchens and ask Ella to give you a wafer. She's been making them especially for you."

"Wafers! Oh!" He turned but at the last moment checked himself and turned back to Philip. "Good bye, my lord," he said with exquisite manners.

"Good bye, Edward."

The little boy thought for a moment, as if he was trying to find the words to express his feelings adequately. Then he sketched a little bow. "Thank you for my mama."

Philip saw Rose's mouth open in a silent gasp, and his own breath caught in his throat. Such heartfelt gratitude! Nothing could have been more touching.

"You are very welcome. It was my pleasure to help your mama and you. And the horse's name is Sapphire," he said, patting the stallion on the rump.

Edward beamed at him. A moment later, he was gone. Silence fell in the courtyard.

"Sapphire. Have you seen your horse, my lord?" Rose chose to tease him, for she could not deal with what Edward had just said. "He is white as snow. Surely Diamond would have been a better name for him?"

He smiled in acknowledgement of the jest. "I know. But he came in a blue caparison, and I just could not resist."

"How long have you had him?" She was sure he had ridden a dark bay stallion in the summer.

"A few days." He planted his gaze into hers, as if he wanted her to understand something. She gulped, understanding all too well. He had thought of her when he had named the horse, recalling how she had named her mare Emerald because of the color of her caparison.

So she had been on his mind in the same way he had been on hers these past few weeks…

The thought was dizzying, and opened new, dangerous possibilities in her mind.

"Edward loves horses. I'm sure you could tell," she whispered.

Philip smiled. “It would have been hard to miss. I was the one riding with him yesterday, remember? I confess I only understood about half of what he said to me, but there was no mistaking the intent. He was ecstatic to be riding a stallion.”

Something flipped inside Rose’s stomach. This was getting worse and worse. She knew Philip had to go, she had told him as much, but she was on the verge of begging him to stay, regardless of what she knew she should do.

“Henry would have been proud of his son,” Philip told her suddenly, his face becoming serious. “He is a delightful little boy, a credit to you. Fortunately, it appears that our friend Chichester didn’t manage to ruin his sunny disposition.”

“Thank you.” It felt good to hear someone else say that Henry would have been proud of Edward. She spent her time wondering what he would think, and this was one of the few certainties she had.

Yes, Henry would have been as proud of their son as she was.

She gave the stallion a pat on the neck. Her fingers itched to touch something, and it was either stroke the stallion or reach out to Philip to draw him into a kiss. That, of course, would not do.

“We often discussed having a child. I thought it would have happened immediately after our wedding, but in the end…” She shook her head. It had not been meant to be. “Perhaps it was fate that he never knew he had given me a child. Our final farewell was painful enough as it was. I can’t imagine how he must have felt going into battle that day.”

“Terrified, probably, and I don’t blame him,” Philip

answered, his voice deeper than usual. “The Lancastrians faced an army of men desperate to take a last stand. Few prospects are more frightening than men who are prepared to die for their cause. It was misty, bitterly cold. It’s not difficult to imagine that Henry would have wished himself a thousand miles away from there, by your side.”

Rose’s hand tightened on the horse’s mane. The picture Philip was painting was too vivid. A bitter taste flooded her mouth.

“How could you possibly know how cold or misty it was?” she whispered. Then the breath left her lungs altogether as a horrible suspicion invaded her. “On which battlefield did you earn your title?” she stammered, feeling all color drain from her face.

Philip ran a hand over his face, cursing his clumsiness. Now he would have to reveal to Rose what he had tried so hard to keep to himself. But perhaps it was inevitable that his tongue should slip. The words had been straining to come out ever since he had found out where Henry had died.

“Mortimer’s Cross,” he said softly, knowing that nothing would make the revelation any less brutal. But he owed her the truth. He had wanted to tell her many times before, but there had never been an opportune time, and it felt good to finally get rid of the painful secret. “I know how cold it was because I was there. In King Edward’s army.”

“But…Mortimer…” Rose choked on the words. If he had been there, he had fought against Henry! Not only that but… “Then *you* could have been the one who killed Henry!”

It was undeniable. Philip had run many men through

with his sword that day, injured dozens of others. One of them could have been Rose's husband. He would never know.

"It is not impossible," he said in a very low voice.

"You… You have known this all along, and yet you dared to come to me, to my bed… I cannot… All this is your fault! I lost my husband because of you, my son lost his father because of you!" Rose screamed, beside herself with shock. "I almost lost Edward because of you!"

She knew these were perhaps unfair accusations, but she needed an outlet for her pain, her frustration. Besides, if the chances that Philip had been the one killing Henry were slim, the possibility still could not be ruled out altogether.

Her eyes widened in horror.

What had she done!

The man in front of her, who had spent the night in her arms, might be the very man who had killed her husband. How could she cope with that idea? How could she live with the knowledge that she had slept with Henry's murderer? Philip's hands, those hands which had coaxed so much pleasure out of her, might have wielded the sword that had put an end to her husband's life, that had made her a widow and made it possible for Baron Chichester to take Edward away from her.

That gaping hole in his skull she still had nightmares about…

Philip might have been the one who had struck the blow.

She ran to the back of the stables to hide before she fell apart, not wanting Edward to choose this moment to run to her with a treat in his hand and a smile on his face.

She would never have been able to face him. How would she ever be able to look at him, now that she had welcomed his father's enemy—possibly his father's murderer—to her bed? She had betrayed her dead husband *and* her son!

Nausea threatened to engulf her.

A moment later, she heard Philip's spurred boots on the stone floor. It was a sound only a man could make, a warrior, a fighter.

A killer.

"Please, Rose…"

"Don't touch me, don't talk to me, and *don't* call me Rose!" She was struggling to breathe and keep panic at bay. The last thing she wanted was to throw her accounts at his feet and complete her humiliation. "I do not belong to you, do you hear?"

"I know you don't."

She rounded on him, his reasonable answer whipping her despair into a frenzy. "You told me not to feel guilty about what had happened between us! How could you say something like that when you knew all along I was bedding my husband's enemy? How dare you!"

How had he had the gall to tell her something like that, all the while knowing he might have killed her husband? Was that what fair and reasonable men did?

Earlier that morning she had thought she'd been unfaithful to her husband, when in fact she had done worse than that—she had betrayed him with a man who could be his murderer. The first time she had bedded him it had been through no fault of her own, so she might be able to live with that knowledge. But last night she had gone into his arms willingly. More than willingly.

Now she was finding out that it was the worst thing she could have done.

Feeling sick with horror and self-loathing, she turned her back on him. Barely a moment ago she had been laughing with him, thinking that she would miss him, wondering how she would bear to be parted from him!

She had been about to beg him to stay and take care of her and Edward! Everything collapsed within her. How would she survive this?

"Leave."

The word was no more than a whisper. She could not say anything else. Praying that Philip would not insist, she waited, eyes blurry with unshed tears. A moment later the sound of his spurred boots disappeared behind the building.

Then the stallion neighed and galloped away in a thunder of hooves.

She finally allowed herself to collapse.

Philip was gone.

****

The smell hit her nostrils and made her stomach heave.

Rose stared at the pike lying on her plate and understood that she would not be able to eat a single mouthful of it. She would not be able to countenance even the sight of fish for months to come. It had been the same when she was pregnant with Edward.

Her heart sank.

She was with child again. There was no mistaking the signs she had missed during her first pregnancy. And once again there was no father to share the news with.

During their passionate night Philip had given her a

child, the child she had claimed to be carrying after their first night together. His mistake had failed to make her pregnant, but his purposeful and very thorough lovemaking had done so. And now she was ruined. A widow finding herself with child would never be considered respectable.

Perhaps she should not be surprised. Perhaps it was a just punishment for her unseemly behavior that day. The loss of her reputation was nothing to the torment raking her soul. People would know her for a woman who had slept with a man outside of marriage, and that was bad enough, but only she knew just how shocking her situation was. Her swollen stomach would be proof of her wanton behavior, but mercifully it would not reveal the depth of her villainy.

No one would know she had welcomed not just any man to her bed, but her husband's killer.

She had shared only two men's beds in her life. Both had given her a child, and neither would know about it.

Rose recoiled at her cowardice.

Henry had died before she could tell him about his son, and she could not change that, but Philip was very much alive, and well. She even knew where to find him. He did not have to remain ignorant of this child he had fathered. She could go and tell him, if she found the courage to. In fact, she probably ought to.

Despite the manner of their parting, despite the horror of having fallen pregnant by a man she should never have bedded and who might have killed her husband, she knew she had to tell Philip. She could not let him ignore something as important as this. The betrayal of Henry's memory was her issue, not his, and the babe in her womb had a right to know its father.

She had once sworn never to meet with him again, but now circumstances had changed. Once she had begged for him to stay away from her, but she had not known she was pregnant with his child at the time. She had promised herself she would not allow herself the indulgence of meeting with him ever again.

But Philip…Philip had made no such promise.

You need never see me again if such is your wish.

He was giving her the power. The decision was hers to make, he certainly had not said he didn't want to see her again, or forbidden her from visiting Wicklow Castle. Though he had seemed loath to be parted from her, he had been surprisingly understanding. His eyes had been soft with compassion and something else, something she preferred not to dwell upon, something akin to longing for her company. Could it be that he would have chosen to remain with her, had she not sent him away so uncompromisingly?

Thank God she had resisted the impulse to ask him to stay! How much worse a blow would it have been to find out about his presence at Mortimer's Cross once they had started to build a life together!

Besides, she was not free to choose another man, even if Philip had not turned out to be Henry's murderer. In her heart she still felt she belonged to her dead husband.

What would he say if he could see her stomach swollen with another man's child? Perhaps he would not be as appalled as she thought. After all, he had told her before going into battle that she should remarry if he died, and find a protector.

"This is especially important if King Henry's army is defeated. You will be the widow of a traitor," he had said on their last night together. "Find someone who will keep you safe." She had nestled herself into his arms and interrupted him with passionate kisses, unable to bear the idea of his death.

How could she envisage the possibility of belonging to another man? They had been married for such a short time, and surely fate would not be so cruel. Having married Henry for love, she could not imagine marrying another for less. She did not want a protector; she wanted a soul mate, a lover, a friend.

But his words had turned out to be eerily prophetic. He had died in battle, been branded a traitor, and she had needed protection. The only thing Henry had never imagined was that his own father would be her worst tormentor. Neither had he imagined that she would choose her second husband for any other reason than to ensure her safety.

But if she chose Philip, she would do so for lust, nothing more. The way he stirred her blood was indecent. That had to account for her craving for him.

Rose clenched her teeth to stop her sigh from becoming a sob as realization hit. No! If she decided to marry Philip, she would not choose him for lust. She would choose him for love. With his child warm inside her, she could no longer delude herself.

She had fallen in love with Philip.

Had she been told about his treachery at the start, she might have been able to fight the feeling, but she had been told too late. By the time she discovered he had been fighting at Mortimer's Cross, she had already fallen for him. The irreparable had happened even before she had taken him to her bed.

In fact, she had taken him to her bed *because* she

had fallen for him, she realized only now.

However strong her longing for a man, she would have resisted it if she had not been in love with him. She had probably started to fall in love with Philip the day he had appeared to her in the mist, the perfect answer to her prayers. But since the moment he had stood up to Baron Chichester and brought Edward home on his horse, she had known deep down that all hope was lost.

She had fallen irrevocably in love with him.

And now that she had his child in her belly, a constant reminder of the intimacy they had shared, she had no idea how to extricate herself from this tangle.

What could have been the best discovery of her life plunged her into a sea of sorrow. How wonderful it would be to carry the child of a man she loved—if the man in question had not killed her husband, and if the feeling was reciprocated. But alas, she could not be certain Philip had not killed Henry, and she knew that what he felt for her was not love. Even though he had helped her in the most significant way possible, he had made it clear he had done so to repair an injustice and put his mind at rest, not because of feelings he might harbor for her.

He had made love to her, but she could not fool herself that he had done so out of anything more than pure desire. He had wanted her that night, his lovemaking had been too passionate for her to doubt it, but she imagined that an unsettling number of women would be able to make the same claim. The fact that he had come to her bed with urgent need did not make her special in any way. Philip was a man, and a virile one at that. He could easily dissociate his feelings and his urges. She had fooled herself into thinking she could do the same, that she could spend the night in his arms and not want more, but it had been a vain hope. She was now forced to admit it.

Even if he had saved her sanity by giving Edward back to her, even if he had bedded her twice, even if he had almost married her, she would not have any role to play in Lord Chrystenden's life. She would be forgotten, along with Lady Hershey and all the others, in a few months if she was lucky, a few weeks if she wasn't.

And it was better that way, for even if by some miracle Philip wanted her, she would never be able to welcome him. How could she, when she could not be sure he had not killed Henry, the man she had once loved?

It would be the ultimate betrayal.

Henry had urged her to remarry, but of course he had not imagined she would end up choosing his murderer… He would never have sanctioned such a union—he would never have allowed his killer to raise his child!

Rose talked to Edward about his father constantly, but she could tell that for him the word was empty. If she remarried, her new husband would become the only father figure he had ever known. It behooved her to choose that man wisely, and undoubtedly Philip would prove an excellent father figure, as good as his own stepfather had been.

But it did not change the facts. She could not betray Henry's memory thus.

She could not have her son raised by the man who had made him an orphan.

Rose shook her head, pushing her plate of fish away from her.

"You are not hungry, my lady?" the servant

enquired.

“No. Please take it all away.”

She had to stop torturing herself before she lost her mind. The sob she had tried so hard to contain burst out of her.

Was she destined to bear the children of men who would never see them grow?

Chapter 11

"Philip! The very man I wanted to see!"

Philip turned with a commendable effort at graciousness but, if the lady walking toward him was visibly pleased to see him, the feeling was far from mutual.

"My dear Isobel," he said nonetheless, tilting his head.

"Tush. Am I really dear to you?" she asked, tapping his shoulder with the fan she held. The gesture, both proprietary and censorial, set Philip's teeth on edge. He did not need to see any more to be certain that she had not changed. "I have a bone to pick with you," she added with narrowing eyes.

"Dear me. Should I be worried?"

The ironic question did not make her so much as blink. "You should. I heard a few weeks ago that you almost got married." She did not elaborate. Evidently, in her opinion the statement was extraordinary enough she could dispense with any more comment. Philip was alone amongst his friends in not having entered the state of matrimony.

"Yes. I almost got married," he agreed smoothly, wondering how she could possibly have heard about his failed marriage to Rose. So few people knew about it. Who had been indiscreet? The disgruntled priest? Emeline? "What of it?"

"What of it!" Lady Isobel's face underwent a dramatic transformation from playful teasing to genuine outrage. "Odious man! Must I remind you that I once entertained some hope that you would offer for my hand?"

"No, you must not. My memory doesn't fail me."

Philip mitigated what he had meant as a rebuke with a smile. He knew the news of his nuptials, even if they had fallen through at the last moment, would have been a blow to her. She had tried to entice him into proposing to her by all the means at her disposal, some more pleasurable than others, but he had never entertained the possibility of making her his wife, and he had most definitely *not* enjoyed her persistence. In fact, it had been the main reason why he had put an end to their affair.

"And may I ask who was the woman lucky enough to attract your attention?" Lady Isobel cooed.

Philip couldn't resist teasing her. She was asking for it, and he was not a man to shy away from giving people what they deserved.

"A penniless widow," he said tranquilly, knowing Lady Isobel would choke on his declaration.

Her reaction was just as strong as he had hoped.

"Indeed! A penniless widow, no less!" she spat. "Next you will tell me she was a woman of no exceptional beauty!"

"I will not." Philip's smile widened. "That would be a lie. She was a rare beauty. I could tell you, however, that she already had a child from her previous marriage."

"Fye! That is preposterous." Lady Isobel was so shocked that for a moment she forgot to pout.

Philip crossed his arms over his chest. He had aimed his answers well.

The idea of him falling in love with a beautiful woman when Lady Isobel took pride in her beauty and was jealous of others, of him choosing a penniless bride when she despised poor people, of him considering marrying a mother when she claimed not to want pregnancy to destroy her body, and offering his hand to a widow when he had told her once that he would never consider marrying anyone who had already been married would incense her beyond bearing. All he needed to make her explode with rage was to add that Rose had manipulated him into this union and that he could not forget the feeling of utter bliss he had felt in her arms.

Lady Isobel, who had tried everything she could to push him for a decision regarding a match between them and gone to extraordinary lengths to be remembered as his most fiery partner, would no doubt take exception to that.

He toyed with the idea of telling her that despite all her artful seduction, she could not compare with Rose, in any way. When given the choice between being handed fruit on a gilded platter or having to pluck it on his own, Philip would always choose to climb the tree. An apple tasted sweeter for the effort that had gone into the procuring of it.

Seeing that she was on the verge of an outburst already, he remained silent. Nothing would be gained from enraging her further. The woman could be quite spiteful, and he wished to put an end to the confrontation as soon as possible.

"And why, pray, did you not marry this paragon in the end? As if I needed to ask?" she sneered, making her meaning clear. She thought he had come to the conclusion that a penniless widow burdened with a child, beautiful as she may be, would never be a suitable choice for a man like him.

"I realized that we were not suited after all," Philip said tersely.

Suddenly he lost the will to tease Lady Isobel, or reveal any of the reasons for the breaking of his engagement to Rose. It felt disloyal to her. What had happened was between them alone, and he just wanted to get rid of Lady Isobel.

"Will you be looking for someone more suitable next time you are looking for a wife, my lord Chrystenden?" she asked with a knowing smile.

"I might," he said, wishing to put this conversation to an end. It was clear that his new title had only rendered him more appealing in her eyes. "I think the future Lady Chrystenden should be someone a bit more prestigious than a nobody burdened with a child."

Lady Isobel chose to understand that his choice would fall on someone like her and gave a little self-deprecative giggle he guessed was meant to arouse him. It only managed to irritate him, but at least this effort at appeasement had achieved what he wanted and sent her on her way. It was all that mattered.

He watched her walk away with undulating hips, and let out a sigh of relief. Talking about Rose had made him strangely wistful, and he just wanted to be alone with his thoughts. The last few weeks had been torture. Not only had she disappeared from his life the moment he had realized there was more to his feelings for her than physical desire, but the manner of their parting had left a bitter taste in his mouth.

He had the unpleasant impression of having handled the situation badly.

Despite what Rose had requested, he would have to go and see her soon for fear of losing his mind. Too many things had been left unsaid, too many questions unanswered. He could not leave things as they were.

"Well, I suppose now I know what you really think of me."

The voice coming from behind the bushes was vibrating with indignation. Philip turned and almost jumped out of his skin when he saw the woman walking toward him.

"Rose!"

Was he dreaming? He had just been thinking that he would have to see her, and she had appeared out of nowhere, as if he had the power to summon her at will. He took in her appearance in one all-encompassing, admiring glance. Dear God, she had never been more beautiful. Her blue dress, the color of which brought out the sparkle in her eyes, hugged her in all the right places and made her figure appear even more voluptuous than he remembered, quite a feat since he considered her the most alluring woman he had ever held in his arms.

"At least now I know what you meant when you said that sometimes overhearing conversations could be useful. It seems that you were right," she said, her voice thick with emotion. "This was most enlightening. Now I know where I stand."

Philip's heart plummeted. She had heard all the awful things he had said about her. As if he had not hurt her enough already…

Rose's heart broke in her chest. Philip had never loved her. This did come as a surprise, though it still hurt, but worse, he considered her a nobody burdened with a child, and he was relieved that their marriage had never taken place!

He had mocked her just to entertain this Lady Isobel, who had delighted in being told just how unsuitable a woman she was.

Heavens, why had she come?

A week ago she had discovered that Philip had been invited to attend a banquet given by the Earl of Estell. His lands were just on the other side of the hill, and by happy coincidence she knew his daughter Anna. It had not been hard to convince her to invite her also. This was the chance she had been waiting for. Meeting Philip there would save her the humiliation of having to go to Wicklow Castle, where she would be recognized by everyone as the woman their master had almost married, only to send her away the very morning of the ceremony in disgrace.

Conscious of her duty toward him, she had finally gathered the courage to come and apprise him of her pregnancy.

When he'd gone for a stroll toward the garden earlier, she had followed in the hope of finding an opportunity to speak to him alone. Unsure of what to tell him, or rather *how* to tell him, for she knew all too well what she needed to say, she had waited for him to reach the bench she had found to support her unsteady legs. A moment later, she had seen him walk toward her. Just when she was about to step out of the shadows, a woman in a tall, utterly impractical but fashionable henin had accosted him, and that had halted her immediately.

It had been impossible not to hear their conversation from where she was. There had been no other choice—had she moved an inch they would have seen her.

So she had been forced to sit there and listen to

Philip telling Lady Isobel that he had narrowly escaped marriage to a penniless widow, an unsuitable wife. Every word had been a dagger plunged into her breast. And then, as if it was not enough, she had heard him all but propose to the woman! It had been unbearable, surpassing in humiliation even the moment Sir Gilbert had found her in bed with a naked man and called her a slut, for she had known even at the time that she was not a slut, whatever he thought.

But this time she did not have that consolation. She *was* a penniless widow with a child, an unsuitable choice to become the next Lady Chrystenden. She just hadn't realized that Philip thought of her that way. Never had he treated her as if he considered her below him.

Until now.

Forcing herself to ignore the way her legs wobbled, she made to walk away. She would not tell him about the child now. If he thought so little of her, he did not deserve to know.

"Rose," he said softly. "Please. Listen to me."

"Thank you, I have heard enough for one evening," she murmured, trying to squeeze past him. Predictably, he did not let her. He planted himself in front of her, blocking the only way out of the garden. Rose could tell he would have been more forceful, but her murderous look stopped him in his tracks.

After what she had heard, she would rather die than let him touch her.

"Rose," he repeated more firmly, the voice of a man not used to being denied. If he was not going to physically restrain her, he was not going to let her go before she had heard him out.

"I told you not to use my name," she reminded him,

knowing the protest would fall on deaf ears. Philip was not a man to be told what to do. "I take it that Lady Isobel is one of your former flames?" Even if the lady had not alluded to their affair it had been obvious from the familiarity she had displayed in front of him that they had once shared a bed. Rose knew that her ragged voice betrayed her animosity, but she did not care. It had hurt to see the kind of women he considered suitable, for she would never be able to compete against such fashionable, haughty ladies. "Do tell me, did you go to her by mistake or by design?"

"You are the only woman I made love to without knowing who I was holding in my arms. I will make sure you are the last one." Incredibly, Rose saw his lips curve in a smile. He was amused! It only infuriated her further.

"Surely you do not mean the last woman ever. You are not yet in your dotage, my lord."

"Thank you. I too like to think I have a few good years ahead of me."

She ignored the taunt. "You must mean that you will make sure never to make love to another woman by mistake, then. I daresay it was humiliating for the great seducer you are to find that you are incapable of telling two women apart. I understand why you would not want a repeat of the performance."

"Making love to you was anything but humiliating," Philip purred, coming closer to her. "And I would give my fortune for a repeat of it."

Rose's heart flipped over in her chest. She had failed to provoke his ire, spectacularly so. He was not ashamed in the least, or even angry. She gulped, recognizing the glint in his dark eyes. No. He was not angry. He was aroused. It had been a mistake to allude to their lovemaking. Her own body had caught alight at the memory and, judging from the smile on his lips, Philip knew it.

Very deliberately he let his eyes wander up and down every inch of her.

"Making love to you was the most satisfying experience in my life, Rose. The pleasure I felt in your arms was bone-shattering."

"You thought I was someone else! I am sure I should not set much store by your compliment, if indeed such crudeness can be considered a compliment!" she sneered, doing her best to fight the warmth spreading through her veins at his words.

He shook his head slowly. "You are misunderstanding me. What happened at Harleith Castle was certainly good, but it was nothing compared to the second time, when we made love in your house, in your bed, when I knew full well who you were, when I saw your pleasure, when you knew who was inside you." His voice stroked over her. "*That* was the most satisfying lovemaking in my life. I think it wasn't bad for you either, if memory serves."

He leaned over her until their noses almost touched. Their noses and their mouths.

Rose licked her lips. She could not help the wanton reaction, and against all reason she hoped Philip would kiss her. She would never make the first move herself, but if he kissed her she would not fight him off. She could always tell herself afterward that he had not given her any choice.

Her body edged forward as desire swelled within her.

What was happening? Somehow pregnancy seemed

to have softened her anger, blunted the horror of knowing who was responsible for making her with child… How was that possible? Two months ago she had been horrified at the idea that she had allowed Henry's murderer into her bed, and only a moment ago she had been filled with recriminations toward him.

But now… He had stepped toward her, and everything had vanished in a haze of lust.

He was still the man who might have killed Henry, but she could not ignore that he was much more than that. He was also the man who had got Edward back for her, the father of her unborn child, the lover she desired more than anyone she had ever desired in her life, the man she had fallen in love with.

None of this mattered, though, because even if she managed to give him the benefit of the doubt for Henry's murder—and it was far from certain she would be able to—he did not want her. Even if she betrayed Henry, even if she forgot her scruples to ensure her unborn child's future, it would still be for nothing. Philip would not want to raise a child with a woman he deemed so unworthy.

"I have to go," she said, doing her best not to sound as distressed as she felt. "I should never have come."

"I disagree," he growled. "You are definitely where you should be. Here with me. But what on earth were you doing hiding in the bushes?"

"I was hoping to attract Lord Jessamy's attention," she said brazenly, not wanting to admit that she had been searching for him. Philip only smiled.

"Oh, no, you weren't. Lord Jessamy is a fool, and well you know it." There was laughter in his voice, the sound of a man sure of himself. Once again she had failed to provoke him. "I think you were hoping to attract *my* attention. When you saw me earlier, your eyes caught fire, and not just because you were angry." His forefinger came to graze the side of her face. "Don't deny it, Rose. You were waiting for me."

When she stayed silent he gave a low grunt.

The sound travelled all the way down Rose's body. Indeed she had been waiting for him, only not in the way he meant. A wolfish smile stretched his lips, revealing his teeth, and she was reminded of the way he had nipped at her flesh while making love to her. Her insides instantly dissolved, and to her shock a whimper escaped her.

Yes, Rose had been waiting for him, Philip concluded with ill-concealed satisfaction. It was the only explanation for the delicious flush spreading on her cheeks and her adorable lie about wanting to attract Lord Jessamy's attention. If he thought for a moment that was true, he would go to the man and incapacitate him there and then.

No one would be allowed to waylay Rose tonight but him.

He had not known she would be present at the banquet. If he had, he would have made sure to find a moment with her alone as soon as he'd arrived. When he had heard her voice, at first he thought he was imagining it. And then he had seen her, even lovelier than in his memory, standing so close behind him. Her eyes were glittering with anger, her chest heaving in indignation, but the fact remained.

She had been looking for him. Otherwise she would never have overheard his conversation with Lady Isobel.

Should he be hopeful? Did it mean she had done

some thinking over the last two months and seen that she could not let her past stand in the way of what they had together? Had she finally freed herself of the guilt of welcoming him to her bed?

He dearly hoped so.

What they had gone through together deserved more than an angry parting. They needed a second chance. Now that everything was out in the open, maybe they would be able to start anew?

"If I was waiting for you, I was ill rewarded," Rose said gratingly. "Your former lover got there before me."

Former lover. Ah. So *that* was what bothered her above everything else. Hope swelled further inside of him. A woman uninterested in him would not have taken exception to him meeting a former conquest.

"Well, Lady Isobel is a notoriously persistent woman. Fortunately I was able to get rid of her reasonably quickly."

"By abusing me!" she hissed, none too pleased with his answer.

"I praised your beauty," he reminded her wryly. Dear Lord, how he had missed her sharp tongue!

"Yes, though I suspect from the smile on your lips that you did so more to upset Lady Isobel and make her see that she had no hold over you than for any other reason."

"Very observant, as always," Philip murmured appreciatively. That was exactly what he had done, only the lady had failed to see it. "Still, I did not lie. I merely made sure to mention it when, I grant you, I could and probably should have remained silent. I did not lie, Rose. You are without a doubt the most beautiful woman I have ever seen."

He all but undressed her with his eyes, remembering how alluring she had looked lying on her bed with her legs spread out for him.

Oh, Lord.

Rose almost collapsed to the floor in a puddle. Only Philip would dare to look at a woman with such naked desire. But though his intentions could not be ignored, oddly, it did not make her uncomfortable. A few men had looked at her with lust, most noticeably Sir Gilbert, but unlike them, Philip didn't make her feel humiliated or soiled, only…beautiful and desired.

Besides she would be surprised if the expression on her face when she looked at him did not reflect a similar intent.

She lowered her eyes. She did not want him to see longing in her gaze; she did not want to feel that way about the man she should never have allowed into her life.

"The revelry is about to start," she mumbled, wishing herself well away from him. Why had she come here tonight? How had she ever thought she would find the courage to speak out? If Philip did not want her, he would not want to hear about a child he had not meant to father.

"I care not about the revelry," he said with his usual bluntness. "I would much rather stay here with you and listen to what you came to tell me. You wouldn't be here if you didn't have a purpose in mind."

But Rose knew she would never speak out now, for she had just realized something. Even if she found the strength to tell him about the child, Philip would not believe her. How had she not thought about it before? Of course he would not believe her! He would think this was just another lie. After what had happened on the beach, he would not fall for the same trick twice, and she could not blame him. Except that it was not a trick this time.

She *was* carrying his child, conceived on the night he had given her son back to her.

It would be unbearable to have him mistrust her word and deny a child of his loins, to hear his cutting remarks and accusations. She would have to do this on her own. She would have to send him away without telling him about this baby.

An image flashed through her mind of his pained face when he had talked about the loss of his daughter, then of his disappointment when she had admitted to not being pregnant. On those two occasions, she had had the impression that, more than anything else, Philip wanted a child to love. The man was a born father. She had seen it in the way he acted with Edward. Her son had not forgotten the knight who had taken him back to his mama on a white horse, as he kept referring to Philip. He had once told her that he wanted to be like him when he grew up.

Rose had found it very hard to keep her tears at bay in front of the little boy—as hard as she was finding it now. Edward wanted to be like Philip, not like his real father. And he would have to live all his life with a stepbrother or sister who reminded him of his mother's shame. What if the two children hated each other like Philip and Gilbert did? How would she bear the knowledge that she had been the one responsible for inflicting such a situation on two innocents?

It had been a mistake to come. It had been wishful thinking on her part to think Philip would want to have anything to do with her. Overawed by the news of her pregnancy, utterly at a loss, she had wanted to believe he would support her and the babe, that he would welcome the news of a child. He might well do, but not with her, a penniless widow, a nobody burdened with a child, as he had just called her.

"I have forgotten what I came here to tell you. In view of what I heard, I doubt it would have been of interest to you anyway."

"You are harsh with me, Rose." Philip's eyes glittered.

"No more than you were with me just now," she retorted. "How could you have been so unforgivably rude? All you would have had to do to make my humiliation complete is tell her my name."

"I would never have done such a thing! I told you, I only wanted to get rid of Lady Isobel!"

"Congratulations. You did, for now," Rose sneered. "But she will be back with a vengeance, as she is now convinced that you are going to propose to her. Good luck. I've heard she is notoriously persistent."

They stayed with their eyes locked for a very long time.

Rose opened her mouth, only to close it again. There was nothing more to say.

Philip's fingers tightened on the hilt of his sword. The hope he had felt earlier had well and truly vanished. If Rose had really been prepared to give him a second chance, she would have understood that he had not meant a word of what he had said to Lady Isobel. And maybe she had understood it. She had not lost her powers of observation. Maybe she was only using the whole thing as an excuse to bring matters to an end between them. That way *he* would be the one at fault, the one responsible for ruining what they could have had, not she.

Her inability to cope with her guilt would not be to blame, and her conscience would be clear.

For weeks he had fought the urge to go and see her, as he wanted to give her the time she needed to come to terms with what had happened between them. Surely she had seen that what they shared was special. Coldness invaded Philip when he understood that however much time he gave her, Rose would never be able to get past her supposed betrayal of her husband, and never allow herself, and them, a second chance.

After tonight, she would never seek him out again.

"I am leaving for Burgundy tomorrow," he said, straightening himself to his full height to strengthen his resolve. It was either that or whisk Rose back to Wicklow Castle and make love to her all night, whether she wanted it or not. "I refused the opportunity to go when I was asked a week ago, but now nothing is stopping me."

The only thing that had kept him from accepting the mission was the hope that perhaps it was not all over between Rose and himself. Now that she had made her opinion clear, he had no reason to stay. A change of scenery was the very thing needed to make him forget her once and for all.

He needed to give himself a chance at healing. It would not happen if he stayed here, hoping to see Rose at every opportunity. Abroad, he would not mistake her for every woman wearing a blue mantle, and there wouldn't be the constant temptation of going to see her at home in the middle of the night and stealing into her room.

"Burgundy!" she exclaimed. "Must you go so far? Isn't it dangerous?"

"What does it matter to you where I go or why?" he snarled back. Was she trying to send him mad, blowing hot and cold this way? One moment telling him she was vying for another man's attention, the next acting all concerned for his welfare, as if she cared one way or the other! "I bid you good night, my lady. I believe Lord Jessamy is waiting for you."

He bowed and left abruptly in the direction of the castle. All around him, laughter filled the air.

Indeed, the revelry had started.

Chapter 12

"Gil, you will never guess who I saw last week ambling in Lady Rothscoff's garden," said Lord Woton.

"Someone I know, I suspect. Otherwise I fail to see how I could answer the question." Gilbert laughed like a man proud of his own wit.

Philip did not bother to hide his irritation. After less than a day, his stepbrother's inflated opinion of himself was already grating on his nerves. He had just come back from three months in Burgundy, where he had taken a momentous decision.

He was going to swap Wicklow Castle for Harleith Castle, and he wanted to implement the change as soon as possible.

The idea had implanted itself in his mind when he tried to find ways to root Rose out of it. It was the obvious thing to do. Not only had Wicklow Castle never truly felt like a home to him, but he would always be reminded that Rose could have been mistress of the place. He could not bear the idea of seeing her everywhere he went. The garden where she had told him about Edward, the great hall where he had watched her eat, the bed where she had slept for two nights, the chapel where they should have been married…

It would be torture.

Besides, he did not want to deny his longing to live at Harleith Castle any longer. It was where he had grown up, and he was fond of the place, contrary to Gilbert, who did not feel anything for his rightful inheritance. Still, he lived there, and Philip did not want to stay away from a place he loved just so he could avoid his stepbrother. So he had offered him a straight swap. His ambitious stepbrother had been only too happy to accept, exchanging his childhood home for a grander residence without having to spend a groat.

The deeds would be drawn soon. In the meantime, Philip would make himself scarce, having no time for Gilbert's antics. Now that he had convinced him to agree to the scheme, he did not have to endure another moment of his insufferable behavior. As soon as he had gone to the village to see that Hettie was well, he would leave. Her term would be fast approaching, and he wanted to give her and Scott a present for the new babe.

He made to open the door, but Lord Woton's next words stopped him in his tracks.

"Your once betrothed, Lady Rose Maltravers," he announced triumphantly. "And it seems she got over her disappointment quickly enough."

"What does that mean?" His stepbrother's voice betrayed a sudden interest in his friend's story, an interest Philip shared a thousandfold. Here was a chance to have some news of Rose. Although he had gone to Burgundy with the express intention of pushing her out of his mind, the whole endeavor had been a resounding failure. Not a moment had passed without him cursing himself for leaving her.

He stilled but did not turn around, not wanting to draw attention to himself. He needed to hear the rest of the story, and the last thing he needed was for Lord Woton to get distracted now.

"She is with child, that's what I mean."

The hand on the door handle tightened its grip until the knuckles became white. Philip willed himself to stay silent, though his insides were screaming in agony. With child!

"Is she really!" Gilbert exclaimed.

"Yes. Five or six months, I'd say. I marvel that she dared appear in public in such a state—because, let me tell you, I made some discreet enquiries, and it appears that the esteemed lady is not married or even betrothed. Would you believe it?"

"I would believe anything of such a brazen woman," Gilbert replied darkly.

His friend did not ask why that might be and carried on his explanation.

"I thought you would like to know what a lucky escape you've had because, my dear Gil, it seems that the lady already has a child by her first husband, something I suspect you did not know when you offered for her hand."

"By God, I did not! And she would have forced the brat onto me once we were married!" Gilbert spat out. "What a devious, rotten thing to do! Forcing a man to raise a son who is not of his getting!"

Philip could almost feel his stepbrother's eyes burning a hole in his back. He was comparing what could have happened to him to what had actually happened to Sir Thomas. Indeed their father had been forced to raise a son who was not of his loins. But Philip wasn't worried about Gilbert's indignation, he had other things to think about.

Rose was with child!

He remembered the look on her face as they had

parted in the gardens of the Earl of Estell. She had seemed on the verge of telling him something but, hurt by what she had overheard between him and Lady Isobel, had thought the better of it.

Now he knew just why she had sought him out after swearing she would never see him again. She had come to tell him she was carrying his child.

For he was certain it was his child. He felt it in his bones.

By Lord Woton's reckoning, she was five or six months gone, and he knew it would be five and a half exactly. As they had spent their night together at the beginning of November, the calculation was simple. It did not occur to him for a moment that the babe would not be his, that she would have gone to another man. Her reaction upon waking up next to someone who was not Henry had made it plain enough that she was not ready to leave her old life behind.

If she had been unable to do so for him, a man she plainly desired and felt gratitude toward, she wouldn't be able to do it with anyone else.

Behind him the two men, oblivious to his musings, carried on their conversation. He moved to the window unobtrusively, eager to hear more.

"I am amazed that you should have considered marriage with such a fast woman, Gil," Lord Woton was saying. "You could not have ignored her insatiable appetite… Why, you told me she agreed to come to your bed as soon as you had proposed, not even managing to wait the week before the ceremony could take place!"

Philip willed himself to calm. Gilbert had told his friend that Rose had been the one eager to consummate their marriage before it was sanctioned? What a travesty of what had really happened! He fought the need to ram his fist straight into the man's jaw. Never had he been more perilously close to breaking his oath to his father and finally giving rein to the hostility he felt toward his stepbrother.

"Good God, I would never have actually married her!" Gilbert sneered. "And now I have found out she had a brat of her own all the while, I am indeed grateful to have had such a lucky escape."

"Why did you propose if you never intended to marry her?" Lord Woton sounded curious and not a little bit shocked at his friend's admission. His outrage was nothing compared to Philip's, however. He had come to suspect his stepbrother's intentions toward Rose were never honorable, but the reality of hearing it from the man's own mouth was even more sordid than he had imagined.

"I would never have married her, but there is no denying that I wanted her in my bed. I have always found her rather desirable, if you must know. You will agree that she is a pretty little thing, if on the feisty side."

"Indeed." Lord Woton nodded his appreciation.

"She would never have allowed me anywhere near her without a proposal, and I am not one for forcing women." He made a grimace as if the notion was abhorrent to him. Philip almost snarled. Trust the man to try and pass off for an angel, all the while exposing his depravity! "In any case, she wasn't a virgin, so it could do her no harm."

Philip made a conscious effort to remain silent and keep his eyes on the landscape in the distance. So Rose had been duped from the start. Gilbert would have bedded her and discarded her. He had never intended to go ahead with the marriage she desperately needed. She would have sacrificed herself in vain. Had he not unwittingly made Gilbert renounce his plans, she would have been humiliated—and nowhere nearer to getting Edward back.

If he was not surprised at yet another proof of his stepbrother's duplicity, it did not make it less despicable. Even his friend seemed to find his arguments dubious, to say the least.

"You would have taken your pleasure with a woman while knowing you would not honor your promise to her?" he asked, trying not to sound too judgmental. "You would have made love to her and announced afterward that you had never intended to marry her? Forsooth, that's harsh."

Gilbert let out a scornful laugh. "Do not fret. I would not have said I never intended to marry her. I would simply have found an excuse not to go ahead with the wedding." There was an uncomfortable silence. It was clear Lord Woton was not convinced this was what a man of honor should do, and Philip was positively simmering with indignation. "As it happens, I did not have to go very far to find my reason for breaking off our arrangement."

"How so?"

"The very night I went to find her, I found her in bed with another man."

Lord Woton almost dropped his cup of ale. "She never dared! In your own house?" Far from defending Rose, he was now incensed on his friend's behalf. In a distant part of his mind Philip registered the fact that Gilbert had at least kept Rose's supposed indiscretion a secret. It was clearly the first time his friend had heard of it.

"Oh, but she did. You can imagine that after that exploit I had no qualms in sending her on her way. My only regret is that I never got the opportunity to take her after all." He gave a throaty, sinister laugh. "However, all is not lost. If she is not above getting herself with child while unmarried, I might try my luck with her again, once the brat is born. She will not have the gall to refuse me, and I will…"

Philip moved so fast that the two men jumped out of their seats, fearing an attack.

"You will *nothing*. I would advise you to leave Lady Rose well alone," he warned in a lethally cold voice. He had heard enough and was about to explode in rage.

"Would you? May I ask why that is?"

"You will have to contend with the father of her child, for one thing."

"Oh, no trouble there." Gilbert waved his hand dismissively. "Given her temperament, I doubt she even knows who he is."

Philip had never felt so wretched. Of course Rose knew exactly who the father was. Him, the man she regretted bedding. The discovery would have been a devastating blow. She would have spent days agonizing about what to do before finally finding the courage to go to him. Despite her personal misgivings, she had elected to do the honorable thing and tell him about the babe, all the while fearing he would not believe her. After what had transpired between them, she would have imagined he would not even want to hear about a supposed second pregnancy… But she had pushed her pride aside and plucked up the courage to come to him.

And then she'd had to sit and listen while he told

another woman how unsuitable she had been!

No wonder she had kept silent. She would have been hurt beyond belief.

"I am sure she does know who the father is," he said between gritted teeth, his insides twisting in self-loathing. "I am sure she tried to tell him but could not bring herself to, in the end. She probably thought he would not believe her."

"If that is the case, he is hardly going to take exception with my indulging in my desire for her. He would first have to hear about it."

"He will if you boast in front of him about having her."

"What are you saying?" Gilbert's eyes darted from him to Lord Woton, whose face had taken on a distinctly gray tinge. Evidently he thought Philip was naming him as the elusive father and dreaded his friend's reaction. "You are not the father of her child, are you, Woton?" Gilbert asked, raising his eyebrows extravagantly.

"No, I…I swear I…"

"He is not the father, *I* am," Philip said none too calmly. "And if I hear any more about your foul intentions regarding Rose or find out that you have been anywhere near her, you will have me to contend with. This I can promise you!"

The silence following his words was as thick as cold porridge.

"You and… Well, I never!" Gilbert looked torn between incredulity and outrage. "Did you hear what I just said about her? Are you still so hot to defend her after being told that she bedded a man on the same night she had agree to see me?"

"As to that, I think we both know she did not *agree*

so much as relent, to ensure you would honor your promise to marry her. She needed a husband, and you knew it. You took advantage of her!" Philip barked. "You knew she was desperate, and you used her situation to indulge your appalling need for domination. She never agreed to anything, but she had no choice. Had you gone to her bed that night, you would have done nothing less than rape her, and you know it."

He was making no effort to contain his fury, and Lord Woton was all but quaking in his boots. Gilbert, however, was not so easily impressed. A lifetime with his stepbrother had taught him he had nothing to fear. However strong their disagreements, Philip had never once raised a hand to him. For the first time, however, he questioned his ability to remain in control. He might well pummel Gilbert to the ground if he said another word.

It was one thing abusing him but quite another to threaten a woman under his protection. Not just any woman but the woman he loved, the woman who was carrying his child.

He loved Rose. It had taken him time to recognize it, but now he knew how completely she had captured his heart.

"Rape her? Come! Some women cannot be raped, women like her, who…"

Philip silenced his stepbrother by taking a step forward, hand at the hilt of his sword. "*All* women can be raped," he snarled. "Just like all men can be torn to shreds. Do you need proof of what I'm saying? I shall be very happy to oblige."

"She was brazen enough to smuggle her lover into her betrothed's castle," Gilbert said, doing his best to mask his fear under a sneer. "You cannot deny that it was breathtaking behavior on her part."

"I won't." Philip gave a side smile when he remembered their lovemaking that night. Rose had indeed taken his breath away. "But it was all a misunderstanding. She never meant to bed that man. She only allowed him to touch her because she thought it was you, coming to claim what you'd had the gall to demand from her."

"A likely story!" Gilbert scoffed. "She never realized that the man making love to her was not the one she was waiting for? And anyway, how do you know this? Have you perchance turned out to be clairvoyant?"

"I know because I was the man in her bed that night."

Lord Woton let out a little embarrassed cough, and it was clear he would have chosen this moment to slip away, had the two men not stood between him and the door.

Gilbert finally stopped smirking and looked at him with raised eyebrows. "You expect me to believe this?"

Philip drew himself to his full height and walked over to his stepbrother until they stood so close to each other that he saw for the first time that his eyes were the same color as their father's had been. Somehow because the expression in them was so different they had always seemed a shade darker.

Years of resentment rose to the surface. All the humiliations he'd had to endure, the pain of seeing Sir Thomas' disappointment when he looked at his son—everything came rushing out of him. He had honored his promise to his father and had not written his stepbrother out of his life, but this time he knew it was over. Something had finally snapped inside him.

In a few days' time, Gilbert would be settled in Wicklow Castle, and then he would wash his hands of him. Forever.

"I do not expect you to do anything save leave Rose alone." For good measure he placed the hand on the hilt of his sword once again. He would not hesitate to use it if his stepbrother ever laid a hand on her. Nothing, not even blood ties, would protect a man who hurt Rose. "I do not for one moment believe your claim that you do not force women, for this is exactly what you did to her, if admittedly by deceit rather than physical strength. Touch one hair on her head, speak ill of her, even, and you will see that *I*, however, am one to use force when necessary. Am I making myself clear?"

Lord Woton let out a shriek of terror. "Perfectly, my lord."

Philip ignored the comment. He hadn't been talking to him. "If I could order you never to see her again, I would, but I'm afraid it is not possible. People will expect to see you at our wedding."

"Wedding?" Gilbert's eyes almost popped out of their sockets.

"Yes. I am going to marry Rose. If she will have me."

With these words he left the room, ran to the courtyard, and vaulted onto the first saddled horse he saw.

He had allowed Rose to talk him into a simple wedding ceremony once, but he was not going to make the same mistake a second time. This time, the wedding would go ahead, and he would show her to the world, pregnant as she was. It would cause something of a sensation, but he cared not. All he cared about was securing Rose's agreement.

He grimaced. It was far from certain that she would give it. Many obstacles stood between him and her acceptance. She would have to let go of Henry, of the guilt she was carrying. She would have to forgive his hurtful words and learn to trust him. She would have to accept what she felt for him, and believe him when he told her that he loved her.

But if she did all that and agreed to marry him, then the ceremony would be as lavish as he could make it. Gilbert would be a guest, as would Lady Isobel. There was no doubt they would unleash their venom, each boasting to anyone who cared to listen that they had almost married the bride and groom respectively, but that would only add to his satisfaction.

He spurred the horse on, desperate to get to Rose and his child.

Oh, how he wanted that child! Just as much as he wanted its mother. How had he not seen it before? It was as if he had been waiting for a trigger, an excuse to finally admit to himself that the feeling of despondency invading him all these months had one simple explanation. He missed Rose and he couldn't live without her.

Because he loved her.

Hearing Gilbert and Lord Woton discuss her predicament had made everything clear in his mind. It seemed that, in the end, he would owe his happiness to his stepbrother. What a turn of events! He let out a snort at the alien notion, then gave a mental thanks to his father. Had Sir Thomas not insisted Philip remain in contact with Gilbert, he would never have been in a position to rescue Rose from him, and they would never have met.

He pushed on, riding as if the Devil himself was in hot pursuit. How would Rose react when she saw him? Not well, in all probability. The odds were stacked against him, but no matter. Philip was not a man to shirk a challenge, and he would do whatever it took to persuade her.

He pulled on the reins so hard the horse reared up, almost sending him to the ground. No. Despite his impatience, he would have to wait a bit longer before he saw Rose.

First there was something he needed to do.

Chapter 13

How on earth had Edward's hat got tangled in the bush?

Rose gave a sigh and stretched her arms up, trying to reach out for it amongst the branches. Just as she closed her fingers on the hat, two arms stole around her waist and two hands came to cradle her swollen belly. So engrossed had she been in the retrieving of the hat that she had not noticed anyone approaching.

She gave a gasp. Immediately a mouth brushed against her temple, and a voice spoke in her ear.

"Fear not. It's me."

It's me.

Such arrogance in those two words! As if she had been waiting for him to appear out of nowhere all this time, as if because it was him he could take her in his arms so peremptorily. Everything screamed at her that she should not allow Philip to take possession of her in such a manner, even if she was carrying his child. She wanted to disentangle herself from the embrace, but she couldn't move. The warmth wrapping around her was irresistible, the comfort it brought her to be reunited with him robbed her of all powers of thought.

She closed her eyes because, yes, to her utter shame, she *had* been waiting for him to appear out of nowhere all this time, *had* wanted him to come to her and take her into his arms like so.

The hold became an embrace, and she barely restrained a sigh. Never had she had Henry cradle the child in her womb, never had she had a man stroke her pregnant belly so. It felt wonderful.

"Why didn't you tell me, Rose?"

The deep, throaty sound made Rose shiver. Her arms fell to her sides, and the hat she had finally caught dropped to the ground. Philip's fingers started to move over her stomach, feeling their way as carefully as if he could touch the unborn baby through the taut skin. It was a caress of breathtaking tenderness, one she had never hoped to feel, but suddenly she stiffened. She did not want to be so easily seduced. He thought all he had to do was come to her, touch her in his exquisite way, and all her grievances would be forgotten.

No!

It was too easy. The last time they had seen each other, he had been unforgivably dismissive of her. The pain his words had caused her when she had been about to reveal the existence of their child was still raw, even months later.

And of course there was the small matter of his having possibly killed Henry…

That alone should ensure she recoiled from his touch.

She pushed his hands away and took a few steps forward, placing herself at a safe distance before she turned to face him, willing herself to be strong, to do what dignity demanded she do. It would never work if Philip touched her. It would be difficult enough to withstand the glint in his eyes, to resist the seductive purr of his voice, without having to fight the longing his caresses provoked inside her.

"I did not tell you because before I could utter a single word I overheard you calling me a nobody and Edward a burden to that arrogant strumpet Lady Isobel!" she all but shouted. "After that I admit I didn't think you deserved to know."

Philip closed his eyes like a man in physical pain, so much so that she almost regretted her words. Almost. But he wasn't the only one in pain.

"I told you, I only meant to tease Lady Isobel and get rid of her, but you are right, I should never have used you or Edward so. That was unforgivable of me, yet another appalling mistake," he said in a voice she had never heard from him before. "I had no idea you would hear it. I didn't know you were there that night. I am sorrier than I can ever say, because without it you would have told me about the babe, and allowed me to take care of you. You wouldn't have had to face this alone."

"I might not have spoken out anyway," she murmured, shaken out of her anger by his earnestness. He sounded genuinely guilt-ridden, something she had not expected. "I might not have found the courage. It took me weeks to finally decide to come and find you, but I was still not quite sure I would be able to tell you about the child once you were actually in front of me."

"Oh, Rose, am I so formidable that you would have dreaded my reaction?"

Rose blinked. She could not believe he was asking her the question. Had he forgotten the icy rage he had exhibited when he had found out about her deception on their wedding day? Not that she did not understand why he would have been so furious, but surely he knew how forbidding he could be when he so wished. Any woman would be nervous at the idea of telling a man she was going to give him a child he never meant to father, and their past history made the prospect of informing him of this pregnancy all the more daunting.

"Why do you think I hesitated in telling you about this child?" She straightened her back in defiance, making her stomach jut forward in the process. With their child between them like a shield, she found the strength to stand up to him and speak her mind. "I do not think you are a fool. You must know why I could not vouch for your reaction."

"Because you feared I would not believe you," Philip said through gritted teeth. To have her doubt him, even if it was fair, was painful.

"Can you blame me for thinking you would dismiss me when I told you I was carrying your child? You and I have some history of deceit and mistakes, have we not?"

His little Rose was unafraid, bold as ever. It warmed him to the pit of his soul to see her so true to herself. This was the woman he loved.

"Yes, we do have a shared history," he agreed, baring his teeth in a smile. "But deceit… Now I know that it was not deceit as much as desperation on your part. As to the mistakes, they are all mine, even if some were unintentional. You certainly have nothing to blame yourself for. I will not hear of it."

Rose opened wide eyes.

"Why are you not angry with me?" she whispered. Once again, and though she was questioning his character, he was being reasonable, generous even, and taking the blame onto himself.

"I am not angry with you because all I can do is marvel at how beautiful you are when your temper is roused," he told her, coming forward. "The more you scold me, the more you appeal to me. I would listen to you all day vituperate against me if you look like this when you do. So upbraid me again, Rose. I know I deserve it."

Rose was speechless. Nothing he was saying was making any sense. He *liked* her berating him? Then she saw how he was looking at her. Anger was definitely the last thing on his mind. His gaze caressed her body, as surely as his hands had, and the gleam in his eyes was that of a…

Of a man in love.

She recognized it, having been lucky enough once before to be looked at in this way.

For a long moment she stared at him, wondering if she was dreaming, hoping she was not.

"Why are you here?" she asked, heart in her throat.

Philip's gaze flicked over Rose's swollen stomach. A more beautiful sight he had never seen. These two people belonged to him. They were his to protect. He had just felt his child under his palm, felt the warmth of Rose's body pressed against him. He longed to feel it all again, needed to feel it again. The woman he loved and the child she was giving him, the two most important people in his life, were in front of him, and he was going to have to conquer them, to show Rose that he deserved them. Forget Mortimer's Cross, St. Albans, Towton—this was going to be the most important battle of his life.

"I heard you were with child. I had to come."

"I fail to see why you would have thought it was any of your concern."

Rose could not resist the provocation, but he let out a burst of laughter. She had not rankled him in the least.

"Any child of mine is my concern, Rose," he said, gazing straight at her.

"Are you so sure it is yours? We have been apart for months. It could be someone else's child."

"It could," he agreed easily. "But is it?"

He took a step toward her, then another, slowly, as if he feared her lashing out at him. Not because he was afraid of any harm she might inflict on him but because he did not want her to distress herself while she was heavy with child. Philip was a protector to the core. When he was close enough, he placed his hand on her stomach, a caress both for her and for the babe inside of her. Rose could not draw away, as much as she would have liked to.

The man was just too magnetic, his touch too pleasurable.

It felt…right. As much as she had tried to tell herself that she could not allow her feelings for him to blossom, that it was wrong to even think about him in those terms, it felt right to be in his arms. She could not deny it any longer.

"Is it my baby, Rose? I believe it is," he said softly, and she was surprised to hear a note of anguish in his voice. He was genuinely hoping she would be honest with him, that the baby *was* his child. His dark eyes were glittering with hope. Had he demanded to be told, acted all high and mighty as she knew he could do, she would have allowed her bitterness to speak out, she would have rebelled against it, but this mark of hope undid her.

He had lost his little girl, and he longed for another babe to love. She could not lie to him after having dashed his hopes for a child once already. It would be too cruel.

"Yes, of course it is your child. I…I haven't been

with anybody else. It was conceived on the night you spent under my roof." She placed her hand on top of his and looked deep into his eyes. The morning light made the molten gold center in them appear to be lit from within.

Philip felt his chest expand. He was going to be a father. He had given her a child.

And she had given his life meaning. For the first time he loved someone, and he was not about to let her go without a fight.

"Yes, it is your child," Rose said, lowering her eyes. "But what difference does it make? You do not trust me. You do not want to marry me, you do not want this baby. You do not love me."

Philip smiled and placed a hand on her cheek. "You are full of certainties about what I want or do not want, Rose."

"Yes. I learnt it the hard way."

She swallowed hard. Countless times she had imagined this very moment.

What if Philip somehow found out about this child and came to demand an explanation? Or worse, demanded to be given the baby once it was born, for him to raise, not her? It was possible. She knew he had regretted not having been able to raise his daughter properly, born out of wedlock as she had been. If the baby was a boy, he would no doubt be doubly determined to keep him. This terrifying eventuality had made her think she would have the strength to resist his charm, but now that he was in front of her she could see this had been a vain hope.

He appealed to her as much as ever, if not more. For now he was not just the most dashing man she had ever met, the man who had made her think that life after Henry was possible. He was also the father of her baby.

And he was the one person who could take it from her.

"Why are you here?" she repeated, her voice breaking at the thought that he could take this child away.

"You are angry with me," he stated rather than answering her question.

"No, I'm… Yes, yes, I am!" she eventually erupted. "I am angry! I am mad, and I am hurt and confused, and wary of you. I am not saying that I am blameless in the whole affair, but you are not innocent either. You lied to me, you hid from me the fact that you fought against Henry!" Finally she asked the question that had tortured her over the last few weeks. Her anger lent her the strength to do so. "What do you want from me? Do you mean to take this child to be raised as your son once it's born?"

A dagger to the gut would not have pained Philip more than this accusation. He had seen how unbearable she had found it to be separated from her son, the lengths to which she had gone to get him back. How could she think he would do the same as that bastard Baron Chichester had done? Didn't she know him at all?

"Rose, after all I did to restore Edward to you, how can you suppose I would want to take your child away?"

"Because it is also yours! You do have a right to it, unlike Baron Chichester." She had the fairness to recognize that Philip would make a good father and genuinely care for the child if he was the one to raise it. There was no mistaking the affection he had displayed when he had talked about his little girl. "And you have so much power. I would never be able to fight you if you decided to claim your rights on this baby. But I…I can't bear the thought of being separated from it!"

She wrapped her hands over her stomach, as if by doing so she could keep it forever.

Philip took her hands in his and forced her to meet his eye.

"Listen to me, Rose. Whatever happens today, I swear I will never—do you understand me?—*never* take this child away from you. Even if it is mine, even if it breaks my heart to leave it behind, I will never do this to you. I will respect your decision."

"What decision? What do you mean, whatever happens today?" she asked, her heart beating loudly in her chest. Why had he come? She still didn't know.

Instead of answering, Philip picked up Edward's hat and gave it a tap to shake the dust from it. He was buying time. Rose's heartbeat increased in foreboding. Philip was not the prevaricating kind. When he had something to say, he said it. There was only one reason why he would delay his announcement.

What he had to tell her would not be pleasant.

"I wanted to come as soon as I found out about the babe, but I made some enquiries before I came to find you, and it took a few days." Philip cleared his throat. Rose cocked her head, dreading what was to come.

"What enquiries?" she managed to breathe.

A pause. "That day at Mortimer's Cross… Your husband Henry fought bravely. In fact, he survived the battle. He only died during the rout afterward, when the defeated Lancastrians fled and were pursued, some as far away as Hereford. I'm sorry."

The words were terrible. Henry had been killed after

the battle, when he might have thought it was all over and he would be able to get back to her. He had been killed for pure spite, not as a fighting soldier but as a hounded dog. She closed her eyes, fighting a wave of nausea.

The grip on her stomach tightened. She needed something to anchor herself to the moment.

"Why are you telling me this?"

"Because I think you ought to know the truth. And because I was still on the battlefield at that time," Philip said, articulating every word carefully. "I remained there once the fighting was over. I refused to go and pursue the fleeing men. The battle was over, and they had lost, but I did not agree with hounding them down. I fight soldiers, armed men, and I defend myself against their blows. I do not strike fleeing, injured men."

Once again he took Rose's hands in his. They were cold as ice. He rubbed them gently. God, what was he doing, making her relive the whole nightmare? There had been no other choice but to tell her what had happened that day, but what if the shock was enough to make her sick, or put the babe in danger?

He pressed on, eager to get to the point of his story.

"I am telling you this, painful as it is for you to hear the truth about your husband's death, because it proves that I cannot be responsible for his death. I now know for sure that I could not have killed or even injured him. Whoever struck the fatal blow, it wasn't me." He spoke slowly, desperate for her to understand what he was saying. "I am absolutely certain I did not kill Henry, and I know you have needed to hear it."

Rose nodded, feeling the huge weight she had been carrying for months ease off her shoulders. So she had not let Henry's murderer into her bed, and she was not about to give Edward a brother or sister whose father had killed his own.

"Yes. Thank you for telling me. I did need to hear that," she breathed. "The guilt was crushing me."

"I know." He gave her hands a squeeze. "I am glad I was able to set your mind at rest. But I'm afraid I had my own selfish reason for making the enquiry."

"What is that?" Rose was confused. Why on earth would he need to know about the fate of her late husband?

"I needed you to know without doubt that I was not responsible for the death of your first husband because I am about to ask for your hand in marriage, and I fear that you would never have agreed even to consider my offer had you not been sure I did not kill Henry. If you refuse me, at least let it be for the right reasons."

Rose's heart had almost stopped at the word "marriage," and she barely heard the rest of Philip's explanation. He wanted to ask for her hand! Was he doing so out of duty, because she was carrying his child? He had wanted to marry the mother of his daughter, unsuitable as she was for him, and he had offered for her once, when he had thought to protect her reputation. Of course, now that he could see for himself that she was truly with child, he would want to do what was right. Philip was nothing if not an honorable man. He would want to protect his son or daughter.

But when he looked at her, the light in his eyes was for her, and her alone. If he undoubtedly wanted to ensure the child's future, he wanted her more. If he had merely wanted to do his duty by her, he would never have gone to the trouble of setting her mind at rest first.

He would simply have married her despite her reservations. But he had wanted her to feel safe in the knowledge that she was not marrying Henry's killer.

And he was right, as usual. As much as she would have liked to accept his offer, she would never have been able to live with herself if she had married the man who might have killed Henry. She would never have been at rest. Doubt would have driven her mad.

"You did right," she murmured.

Philip's eyes sparkled in hope. "Does that mean…?" He knelt at her feet, the picture of love and devotion.

He was waiting for her decision. Rose's heart pounded in her chest. What should she do? What would Henry say? Would he give his agreement to the match?

Yes.

At that precise moment the clouds parted, flooding the meadow with sunlight. Something exploded inside her, and she knew she would accept. She would finally be able to put her doubts at rest.

"Tell me you will marry me, Rose. I fear for my sanity if you do not." Philip sounded on the verge of losing control.

"You know I do not come on my own." She stroked her swollen stomach. "There is this baby, of course, but there is also…"

Philip placed his hand on top of hers, interrupting her. "Edward will be my son. It will be my honor to raise him as mine, if you agree. I love the boy already. How could I not, when I love his mother so? I realized how I felt for you the day I saw you reunited with him. You were so…" He shook his head. "I had never seen anyone so full of love. It moved me. I gave you your son back, and that same day you gave me a child. I think it is very fitting."

Rose could not speak for emotion. She watched Philip look at her stomach in wonder. She could tell he was not seeing a rounded belly but his baby already.

"The child is due in July."

"I know. I was there at the conception, and believe me, I remember everything about that night," he told her with a breathtaking smile. She reddened, also remembering. "I had worked it out for myself. July, how serendipitous. A year after our first meeting." He let out an incredulous laugh and got back to his feet. "God's bones, I never thought I would ever say so, but I am actually grateful to Gilbert. If he had not forced you into his outrageous bargain, we would never have met."

She smiled. "Your mistake ended up being the best thing that could have happened to us."

Philip brushed his finger over her cheek. "I never saw what happened that night as a mistake, my love. A misunderstanding, but never a mistake."

Rose stood on her tiptoes and placed her lips onto his. The kiss, tentative at first, soon became so passionate that it stole her breath away.

"Forgive me," Philip rasped, wrenching himself away from her. What was he doing? He had all but crushed her and their child in his arms. It would have been uncomfortable.

"You're completely forgiven if you are going to kiss me like that."

"There is something I need to ask you. Did you like Wicklow Castle very much?" he asked her, running his thumb along her bottom lip, shiny and swollen from their kiss.

Rose gave a shaky laugh. "Is that the only thing you

can think of right now?"

"No." The dark eyes gleamed. "But the other thing will have to wait until I have carried you to your bed. I think you might object to me lifting your skirts here in the meadow."

Her mouth fell open. He was so…scandalous.

"Why are you asking me if I liked Wicklow Castle, though?" she asked in a breath.

"Because I have given it to Gilbert. I have always wanted to live at Harleith Castle, and I thought he would be only too glad to swap with me. He was, but now I see that I should have asked you beforehand. If you prefer, we can…"

"Philip," she interrupted him. "I care not where we live as long as we are together and you put sheepskins on the chairs. I rather liked that."

"Did you?" he growled. "Then I shall cover every conceivable surface with sheepskins, so I can lie you on them and make love to you."

She gave a tinkling laugh. "I will hold you to that promise."

"My God, Rose, I never thought you could get any lovelier, but…you are glowing," he said reverently, as if he could not believe his luck at holding her in his arms and being allowed to claim her as his own. It was a feeling she understood too readily. She could hardly believe Philip was holding her, cradling their child at the same time, and making them both his.

Now they would never be parted.

"You are mine." They spoke at the same time.

"Yes, I am yours," they answered in unison, smiling at each other.

One, forever.

Epilogue

"It's me, my lady, Philip Stephen Whitlock, Lord Chrystenden, your husband," Philip whispered, lifting the covers to enter the bed next to his wife.

Rose let out a giggle. "Really, there is no need to state all your names and titles!" she chided, turning to face him. "As if I would not recognize you and allow a stranger to come into my bed and make love to me just because it was dark!"

"I know, you have to admit it is unlikely." He placed a kiss on her naked shoulder. To his delight, she had taken to sleeping naked since their wedding day. "But one cannot be too careful," he murmured against her skin. "Such misunderstandings have happened before, or so I have heard."

"Have they?" she asked, smiling in turn. "What happened to the hapless couple, I wonder?"

"I dare not tell you. It is a story too lewd for delicate ears. But I suppose I could *show* you what happened." His hand snaked its way along her spine to come and cup her buttocks. "Do you want me to?"

"I think you want to show me, irrespective of what I want," Rose said, her breath catching as she felt his hardness swelling between them.

"Mmm, yes, I do want you, I cannot lie," he purred. "But unless I am very much mistaken, so do you." His thumb brushed against an already hard nipple. "I know my wife. And I know when she wants me."

"So stop talking and do something about it!"

"As you wish, Lady Chrystenden," he answered in a dark voice. He moved, and Rose found herself underneath her husband before she had time to blink.

"How did your story end, then?" she asked, the last word transforming into a gasp when Philip surged inside of her, filling her in one effortless stroke.

"The man bedded the woman by mistake. He thought she was the bold new conquest who had pursued him shamelessly, and she took him for the rogue who had dared to ask her to give herself to him."

"Oh dear, how inconvenient for them." Rose chose the word he had once used to describe the situation. She saw that he recognized the allusion when his lips stretched in a lazy smile.

"Inconvenient. Yes, that's one word for it. But do not feel too sorry for them. The man ended up marrying the woman." Philip withdrew from her and stayed still for a moment, locking eyes with hers. "She gave him two wonderful children."

Rose felt her heart explode in her chest. The morning of their wedding Philip had adopted Edward, and the little boy who had been born three months later was treated no different to him.

"So they lived happily ever after?" she asked, her voice taut with emotion.

"They did." He filled her again, slowly, deliciously, burying himself to the hilt in her quivering flesh. Then he took her mouth in a lingering kiss. Rose reached around his neck to draw him even closer.

"I love you."

"I love you too. Now let me finish what I was doing,

because you asked me to show you what happened that night, remember?"

Rose smiled. "Yes. Please, show me. Everything."

A word from the author…

I am passionate about history and romance, which seemed to be the perfect combination to start writing my own stories. Being a stay-at-home mum gave me the incentive to do so in earnest.

As far back as I remember, I have always loved reading and writing. I fell in love with the Middle Ages at about age nine when during a history lesson we were taught about the Hundred Years War. A mental picture of a beautiful lady atop the castle battlements with her veils fluttering in the breeze, staring into the distance at her lord riding away to battle, struck my imagination and, once and for all, I had fallen in love!

As a French native married to a Welshman, I am knowledgeable and passionate about both our countries' histories and keen to feature them in my stories.

Visit me at:

virginiemarconato.com

Thank you for purchasing
this publication of The Wild Rose Press, Inc.

For questions or more information
contact us at
info@thewildrosepress.com.

The Wild Rose Press, Inc.

Ingram Content Group UK Ltd.
Milton Keynes UK
UKHW020922100323
418370UK00014B/952

9 781509 247141